Comic Shop Mysteries Book One

The Uncracked Code
FEATURING *KOMODO JONES*

To the 'Amazing' Laura + Eryk,
Love from
Tamara Macfarlane
x

For Mum, Dad, Roy, Lily and Xander – thank you

xxxxx

T.M

To My mother, Julia Mapondera who is quite the real life Komodo Jones

EM

Acknowledgments

Thank you to Jon Appleton, Roy Johnson,
Ken Wilson–Max and Martin West

Comic Shop Mysteries Book One

The Uncracked Code

FEATURING **KOMODO JONES**

Tamara Macfarlane and Roy Butlin

Illustrated by **Eugene Ramirez Mapondera**

troika

Published by TROIKA
This edition first published 2018
Troika Books Ltd,
Well House, Green Lane, Ardleigh CO7 7PD, UK
www.troikabooks.com

Text copyright © Tamara Macfarlane and Roy Butlin 2018
Illustrations copyright © Eugene Ramirez Mapondera 2018

ISBN 978 1 909991 65 1

1 3 5 7 9 10 8 6 4 2

Printed in Poland

Endmatter
Tamara Macfarlane and Roy Butlin
ABOUT THE AUTHORS
You can visit Tamara's website www.moonlaneink.co.uk

Acknowledgements

VWOOSH!

I'M HERE; ARE YOU SURE HE'S ALONE?

DON'T WORRY, ALL CLEAR

CRASHHHHHH!!

WHAT DID YOU DO?

I THINK IT'S IN PLACE. HE LOOKS DIFFERENT

IT MIGHT TAKE A WHILE TO KICK IN. DON'T WAIT YOU NEED TO GET OUT OF THERE

BUT WHAT IF IT DIDN'T CONNECT? SHOULD I DO IT AGAIN?

YOU'VE DONE ALL YOU CAN, KOMODO. JUST DROP THE CAMERA ON THAT TABLE, THEN GET SAFE.

CLICK!
CLICK!
CLICK!
BEEP!!

ALSO, WE'VE STILL GOT THAT CHEMISTRY ESSAY TO FINISH FOR TOMORROW

AGH, STUPID HOMEWORK - CAN'T YOU INVENT ANOTHER SERUM TO MAKE THEM THINK WE'VE ALREADY DONE IT?

SHE NEEDED THAT MONEY SHE NEEDED THAT LOCKET SHE'S SCARED IN HER OWN HOME, I MADE HER SCARED... I MADE HER AFRAID... SHE CAN'T SLEEP. I TOOK THAT FROM HER... HOW COULD I TAKE THAT FROM HER?

SNIFF !
SNIFF!
SNIFF!

GRAN! YOU'RE SUPPOSED TO BE ASLEEP!

KAY? WHY WERE YOU JUMPING OFF BUILDINGS? THAT DOESN'T LOOK SAFE TO ME.

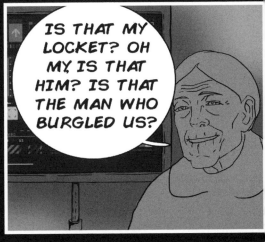

JUST UM, TRYING TO KEEP THE CITY SAFE

IS THAT MY LOCKET? OH MY, IS THAT HIM? IS THAT THE MAN WHO BURGLED US?

WHAT'S WRONG WITH HIM? DID YOU DO SOMETHING?

WE.. I.. MADE AN EMPATHY SERUM, AND KOMODO SHOVED IT UP HIS NOSE

.... WHAT DO YOU MEAN 'EMPATHY SERUM'? DO YOU MEAN HE'S NOW FEELING WHAT I'M FEELING?

YES, EXACTLY, WE DEVELOPED IT FROM KAY'S BLOOD. SHE'S GOT EXTRA STRENGTH AND ... STUFF

GOODNIGHT YOU TWO

GOODNIGHT MRS SMITH

GOODNIGHT

TO BE CONTINUED...

You could be a hero.

You might just be waiting for your moment.

*The moment when you stand strong
in the face of fear.*

*When you discover who you are,
who you are meant to be.*

When you take control of your own story.

*If you asked Coco which moment was hers,
she might say it was the day of the theft.
For Zac, it came later.*

But let's start here ...

Comic Shop Mysteries
by Tamara Macfarlane

BOOK ONE

KOMODO JONES

AND THE UNCRACKED CODE

KOMODO JONES

AND SAM WILSON IN...

KOMODO JONES VS HERSELF

ISBN 978-1-909991-65-1

CHAPTER ONE

Coco needed a wee. This was not, on its own, unusual. She seemed to spend an awful lot of her life hopping from foot to foot, or running down corridors trying to find a loo. It was just that, usually she wasn't being made to stand and wait outside in the street.

Coco glanced in through the window of her mother's shop, Cosmic Comics. She could see the sign for the toilet; it was that close. She looked in through the window of The Comic Café next door and thought about the superhero-themed public loo in there. Before she could stop them, her eyes rolled up longingly towards her flat, directly above the shop, containing another perfectly useable bathroom. Knowing that they were all so close made her even more desperate.

She tried to think about something else.

If this were a scene in a comic, Coco thought, I would not be here waiting for a late delivery van. I would not be curling my toes up to try to stop thinking about how much I really need the loo. I would not be staring anxiously into my shop, seeing loads of customers staring back at me impatiently.

Crowds of people dressed up as characters from the *Forbidden Galaxy* series were queueing up inside, waiting for the author signing to start. Erica North, internationally popular author and illustrator, was inside, pen in hand, poised to sign comics. Coco checked off the ingredients for a successful signing in her head: the shop was open, the author was there, the staff were at the tills, the fans had all arrived … Cosmic Comics had held hundreds of massive author signings before, but never, ever without the comics!

Her best friend Zac waved from the The Comic Café, where he worked with his step-dad, Ed. They seemed to be massively busy too. Coco tried to signal, 'Can you come out here instead of me so I can go to the loo even though I know you're really busy too,' but it obviously just looked as though she was waving, because he just smiled and waved back, before rushing off to serve more of his customers.

It started to rain.

'Stupid van, stupid delivery company, stupid me-for-not-going-before-I-came-outside-to-look-for-vans-that-aren't-here.'

As much as they desperately needed the comics for the event, Coco was even more excited about some of the other new issues that were in the late delivery – especially the latest *Komodo Jones*.

Komodo was her and Zac's all-time, absolute favourite superhero – not as well known as some of the other heroes, there were no films or TV shows and there had only been a couple of issues a year but today, *finally*, a new issue was due. She and Zac had been talking for weeks – months, even – about what might happen, and the best part was that today was only Thursday; they still had three whole days of half-term left to enjoy every detail. There were hints in the previous issue that something would happen in this one that would change Komodo's life forever.

But we'll never know, if this van doesn't arrive! Coco thought. If I was a superhero, I wouldn't have to wait here, uselessly hoping that the next thing around that corner was a delivery van ... I'd leap up the building, climb high on the roof and perch like a mighty eagle, waiting to dive.

The scene began to ink itself out across Coco's imagination ...

Suddenly from the roof, I spot the van. It's trapped in traffic, far in the distance ... Only I can get the fans what they are all waiting for. One giant leap and I'm swooping above the city through the clouds. I spiral down. The ground rushes towards me. Four perfect, impact-controlling rolls and I'm under the van. I lift it above my head and take off with it like a bullet, high above the jammed roads.

I burst back out of the clouds. The crowd goes wild. One quick tip of the van and the back doors swing open. Out pour dozens of comics, and — why not — loads of giant doughnuts!

A quick nod to the applauding crowd and I disappear. My job here is done ...

'Coco!' Zac gave her a not-very-gentle nudge back to the real world.

 'Umm, oh, sorry,' Coco shook her head. 'What did you say?'

'I said that your mum called the delivery people again and they just keep saying that the van is on its way. "Very soon" apparently. And I brought you this.'

He handed her an umbrella.

'Oh great, thank you! I was just thinking about how, if I could fly and carry vans and there were doughnuts –'

'Sorry, Coco, tell me later; I just wanted to check you were okay. It's crazy-busy in there – I have to get back to help Ed!'

Zac headed back into the café.

As he disappeared, Coco remembered again that she was bursting for the loo. She had totally forgotten while they were talking. 'Argh!' She stamped with frustration.

She tried hopping from foot to foot and then walking up and down to try to forget about it. There was no way that she could leave her post. This would never happen to Komodo Jones.

Just as Coco was sure that she couldn't hold on for a second longer, she heard a huge cheer surge up from inside the shop as the van swung around the corner. It screeched to a halt in a puddle, soaking her even more.

Inside, Cosmic Comic's shop assistant, Sasha, emerged to help with the delivery. Her height and confidence magically parted the crowd. She slid out of the door, picked up bundles of the comic and carried them back in. 'Everyone please take a step back,' she said, restoring calm. She grinned at the dripping Coco and dropped the comics behind the counter, where Coco's mum, Emma, was waiting. 'We need two queues, please. Pre-orders on the right, new customers on the left.'

Coco made a quick dash for the loo, but luckily was back on duty only moments after the first few comics had been sold. She unpacked her and Zac's copies of *Komodo Jones* from the top of the second box and stashed them safely under the counter. Taking out the customer orders, she ticked them off and put them into the rack in alphabetical order. Her mother worked the right-hand till. Sasha served the queue on the left.

Two hours later, the final customer was served. Emma turned the sign in the door around to 'Closed'.

Coco didn't want to waste a second. She grabbed Zac's copy of *Komodo Jones* along with her sketchbook. 'I've got to get this to Zac. See you both later.'

'Coco,' Emma called after her, 'don't forget, you promised to show Grace around at six o'clock. You've only got ten minutes.'

Why? Why? Why did I promise that? Coco wondered to herself.

On any other day, at any other time, Coco and Zac would have leapt at the chance to show off every last tiny supervillain model and cartoon-painted wall in the shop and café. Just not now, and not Grace!

Grace's mum, Alannah, was an old friend of Emma's from before Coco was born, but Emma had looked as surprised as Coco when they'd both arrived the previous evening.

Alannah was lovely – funny, silly – and she made Emma laugh so hard that Coco thought her mum would actually fall off her chair. The two of them had been chatting practically all night, telling old stories and old jokes. Even though Coco didn't get all the jokes, it was lovely seeing her hard-working mum relaxed and giggling. But Grace was a different matter.

'OK, Mum,' she shouted back. 'I'll meet her back here in ten minutes.'

Stepping away from the desk, Coco ducked between the model planets hanging from the ceiling. She jumped from star to star across the Milky Way that she and Zac had painted on the floor last summer. Knowing that she was far too old to find it so much fun, Coco checked no one was watching her. Stepping off the edge of the painted universe, she ran her free hand along four bookcases, packed with space-themed comics, alien figures and model UFOs, before stopping with her face and toes pressed up close to the shelves of the end bookcase. Reaching up to the third shelf, Coco pressed down on the head of the fifth mini droid to the right. With a quiet click, the catch released and the bookcase began to revolve.

The hidden door that linked Cosmic Comics with the café kitchen next door never stopped thrilling Coco, no matter how many times she and Zac passed through it. They'd set the droid locking-mechanism up themselves so that even Ed and Emma didn't know how to use it.

In half a spin, Coco was in the kitchen of The Comic Cafe. The smell of warm doughnuts and cheese toasties hit her before the door clicked into place.

THE COMIC CAFE

MENU

TODAY'S SPECIALS

- INTERGALACTIC GATEAU
- CHEESY SHARKS
- MAN ON THE MOON TOASTIES
- BLACK HOLE DOUGHNUTS
- COMIC BOOK CROISSANT

'Zac, I've got your comic and I'm taking some cake,' Coco shouted to Zac as she grabbed a slice of brightly-coloured marbled sponge with silver icing on her way out to the counter. She glanced at the label and snorted: 'Intergalactic Gateau, baked mainly by Martians.'

The café was packed. Every table and chair in the entire place was occupied. Ed delivered food at a pace that defied time. He was almost a blur as he darted between tables and in and out of the kitchen.

Scribbling down the order he was taking as fast as he could, Zac smiled at his friend and hurried over to her at the counter.

'It nearly cost me my life,' Coco grinned, thrusting the comic at him. 'The crowd was wild!'

'Bet it'll be worth it!' Zac put down his order pad and pen, took the envelope with both hands and carefully wiped cake and icing from the edges with his sleeve. 'I wish we had time to read it now. It's been insane in here. Ed and I haven't stopped. How's it been next door?'

'Manic!' Coco replied. 'Mum's only just closed the shop. From the look of it, everyone must have got their comics signed and come straight in here to read them.'

'Complete craziness!' Zac said. 'Its great!'

Coco glanced at the clock. 'Look, I need your help. I've got to show the daughter of one of mum's friends around.'

'You know your way around your own shop,' Zac said. 'You practically drag strangers off the street to show it to them. Why do you want me there?'

'Grace is scary! When I met her last night, she sized me up like I was prey.' Coco picked the icing off her cake. 'She makes me nervous I'll say something stupid or trip over or something. Please come with me. You're good with people. They like you.'

'You'll be fine!' Zac reassured her. 'I promised I'd help Ed out until closing time. That's another hour. And then I am doing nothing until I have read this comic from cover to cover!'

'No way! You can't read it without me! And you have to help me – I'm supposed to be with her now! She's probably burning the place down with her evil eyes or something ...'

'Impossible! Look at this place,' Zac said. 'Ed will never let me go.'

'Nothing's impossible,' Coco said with a grin. 'Ed!' she called. 'Please can I borrow Zac? Just for ten minutes? I'll bring him straight back. And then I'll come and help too.'

'OK,' Ed said, looking up from the sandwich toaster. 'Zac, you could do with a break. But please don't be long. I'm already behind with the orders.'

'Do you ever take no for an answer?' Zac said, laughing as he followed Coco back through the hidden door.

CHAPTER TWO

'Let's get this over with as quickly as possible,' Coco whispered to Zac.

'Talk really fast,' Zac replied. 'If you get through this in under five minutes we might have time to skim read *Komodo.*'

Coco unlocked the front door of Cosmic Comics at high speed to let Grace in. 'Hi,' she said. 'This is Zac. His dad runs The Comic Café next door.'

'Will this take long?' Grace asked. 'I'm only here because Mum told me to wait for her. I've got a dance class in half an hour. She's picking me up from here in fifteen, so if we really have to do this, make it short.'

'Don't worry, I'll do the speed tour.' Coco raised her eyebrows at Zac in relief and led Grace over to the centre of the shop.

'Starting here with past worlds, future worlds, parallel worlds, utopias and dystopias, TV tie-ins, film tie-ins, sequels, prequels and spin-offs. Over here are the first editions, special editions, limited

editions, collaborations and inter-world creations …'
Coco swept her arm across a huge area of the shop.
It was crammed from floor to ceiling with everything
superhero-themed, from pencils to pinball machines.
It was a riot of colour, a carnival of comic merchandise.
'And over here we have the superhero section, also
including supervillains, super pets, sidekicks, sidekicks
who become superheroes, sidekicks who become
supervillains, super pets who switch sides …'

Coco paused to breathe.

'And at the back,' Zac cut in to help her out, 'is
the games and gallery section. In there's a jukebox,
Space Invaders, Pac-man and, most importantly, all
the really, really rare editions. It's where the most
beautiful comic in existence is kept – a one off *Komodo
Jones*, hand-drawn original. The very first! The
author wasn't planning a series at this point, so it
doesn't even have a proper title. It's just called *Komodo
Jones*!' My mum gave it to me when I was four. It's
right at the very back, in an alarmed case.'

'Do you want to see it?' Coco asked Grace.

Completely ignoring Coco, Grace slithered into
a nearby chair. She reached into her bag and
pulled out a fashion magazine. Her long, painted
fingernails began to flick through the pages.

Zac glanced over at Coco and rolled his eyes with a

look of disbelief. She mouthed, *'See?!'* back at him in reply, before getting distracted by a life-size cut-out of Komodo Jones that had been knocked over in the rush of customers earlier and taken a display of action figures with it. The cardboard figure had Komodo in full dragon-lizard armour on one side, and on the other as her regular student self Kay Johns. Coco straightened her up.

'We need to get back to the café.' Zac waved the unread comic at Coco pointedly, 'I think I can hear Ed calling.'

'Two seconds while I pick up these models!' Coco said, scrambling on the floor and searching under shelving for escapee action heroes.

Lowering her magazine slightly, Grace looked straight at Zac, admiring his easy skater style.

'Why do you have to go and work?' she asked. 'Why doesn't your dad just pay someone to help? And why do you call him Ed if he's your dad?'

'Because I always help out in the school holidays, and ... because I like working there.' Zac stumbled, taken back by the sudden interrogation. Grace hadn't appeared to be interested in anything except herself and her magazine. 'Well, technically, Ed is my step-dad, but he's the person whose always been here looking after me.'

Zac wondered why it mattered to him that Grace knew this.

'I've had three step-dads. The last one of them has just left too. Thank God. He was *soooo* boring! So where's your real dad?' Grace asked.

'Ed *is* my real dad,' Zac said.

'You know what I mean,' Grace said, ignoring the slightly impatient note in Zac's voice. 'Where is your real *biological* dad?'

'I don't know,' Zac answered. 'He left when I was a baby.'

'Did he get fed up with all this cartoony stuff?' Grace smirked, casting her scornful gaze around the shop.

'I doubt it,' Zac replied. 'No one could get bored of this.' As he took in all the brilliant things around him, Zac saw that Coco had moved to the galaxy section and written 'Grace is an alien' in ultraviolet pen on the wall. The letters glowed purple behind Grace's head as Coco shone the special torch on them. Zac suppressed the urge to laugh.

'What about your mum, then?' Unused to not being the centre of things, Grace waved her hand at Zac to regain his attention. 'Apparently, your mum, my mum and Coco's mum all used to be in a band together. I've seen photos of them all. So where is your mum now?'

Zac's amusement evaporated at the mention of his mother. His face fell. 'Coco! We need to go!' He headed for the revolving bookcase without waiting for her.

Coco jumped up and ran to join him. With a quick glance to check that Grace wasn't looking, Zac reached for the droid. Leaning back on the bookcase as it clicked into place in the café kitchen, he took a deep breath.

'Don't worry about me. I'll just see myself out then, shall I?' They heard Grace's sarcastic voice scratch through the walls.

Coco rested a hand on his shoulder. 'Sorry, Zac.'

Ed stuck his head into the kitchen. 'I thought I heard you. Coco please turn the sign to "Closed",' he begged. 'Zac, table seven have been waiting forever for the bill. They'll be as glad to see you as I am.' Zac grabbed the opportunity to escape.

Coco joined Ed to help clear the tables. 'We've had a busy afternoon, thanks to your event,' he smiled. 'But how's everything else? Have you and Zac finished writing your latest Salamander strip?'

'It's almost done,' Coco said, smiling at the thought

of her and Zac's own fanzine. 'I'm just having trouble working out the ending of this month's mystery. A boy's been framed for something he hasn't done by some kids who've got it in for him ... Hang on, hang on ... *I've got it!*' Coco ran and dropped the dishes into the sink. 'Back in a sec.'

Ed shook his head affectionately as Coco ran back through the revolving door to the bookshop to grab her notebook. She ran straight into Grace, who was leafing through it.

'I thought you had to go?' Coco said, as calmly as she could after spotting the notebook in Grace's hands.

'Mum's late as usual. Don't think I want to be stuck here with nothing to do,' Grace replied.

Trying not to point out that Grace must be the only person in the world who could find nothing to do in a shop stuffed with comics, Coco asked for her notebook back.

'Why do you want it?' Grace stood up and dangled it above Coco. 'It's full of made-up stuff. Who names a detective after a lizard, anyway? Salamander? That's just weird.'

'You wouldn't understand. Please. Just give it back.' Coco tried to grab it. How she wished that she had a superpower. Or even just some normal power. Komodo would have drop-kicked Grace to the floor in a second.

'Superheroes are so childish,' Grace sneered. 'It's all stupid tights and terrible capes. They're not even fashionable.'

'They're helping people. They're fighting for truth and justice. Does it matter what they're wearing? Isn't what they're doing more important?' With that, Coco lunged forward and snatched the notebook from Grace's fingers. 'Actually, forget it, there's no point trying to explain it to you.'

'Well,' Grace looked at Coco's pale face, unkempt hair and mismatched clothes, slowly and deliberately. 'I can see that there's no point trying to explain fashion to _you_.'

With all the power within her, Coco held herself back from physically pushing Grace back out of the front door.

Grace's phone buzzed. 'It's my mum – I need to go.' She tottered out on her stupidly high-heeled shoes.

'Don't rush back,' Coco whispered, making a swift retreat to the café.

Most of the customers had gone by now and the person at the last table was getting up to leave.

'So, you've got the ending?' Ed asked. He looked

up from the sink and noticed Coco's face. 'Hey, what's up?'

'Grace is a nightmare. Please tell me that they're leaving soon.' Coco flung her notebook down.

'I'd love to,' Ed said. 'But when I saw them arrive at the shop yesterday, it looked as though they were planning to stay for a while. Your mum and Alannah go way back.'

'Grace is like one of those super-ugly aliens that disguise themselves as a beautiful person, mixed with a starving toad and then shoved in a pair of leggings,' Coco said. 'First, I have to give up my room to her. It has my desk in, which has my drawers in, which have all my things in – my pens and books and comics and, well, everything. It's *my* room. Grace should be on display in the supervillain section ... and instead, she's sleeping in *my* bed!'

'Did she eat your porridge too?' chipped in Zac from behind the counter. Coco tried to glare at him and not to smile, but ended up doing both.

'That does not sound good.' Ed put a large chocolate fudge brownie milkshake down in front of her. 'Try that. It's a new recipe called The Volcano.' He stood back and watched as Coco took a long slurp on the straw. Her eyes lit up.

'*Wow!* That is the best thing that you have ever made!' Coco drank some more. 'Without a doubt.' She took another sip. 'Zac, you have to try this. Get to the caramel bit.'

'Try it?' Zac asked sticking his head out of the kitchen, 'I just made it for you, you daft warthog. I've been working on it for weeks. Is Ed taking credit for my amazing creations again?'

Grabbing a straw, Zac came to join her. 'Yep, definitely the best thing on the menu,' he teased Ed after drinking half of it down in one go.

'It's not on the menu yet …' Ed replied.

They all looked up as the front door jangled. The landlord, Mr Haines, strode in without a hello. 'Ed, we need to have a conversation.'

'Sure, Mr Haines, what can I do for you?' Ed asked. He closed the till.

'I'm going to have to double the rent from the beginning of next month. I've told you before, lots of people want this site. I can't run it like a charity.' Before Zac's step-dad could respond, he continued. 'You've got one week to sort things out, No rent. No shop.'

'A week? That's not what your letters said!'

'Don't make me out to be the bad guy, Ed. This is

business.' And with that, the landlord walked back out. The door banged shut behind him.

'That wasn't much of a "conversation". Run it like a charity!' Ed fell back into a chair as though the shock of the news had pushed him down. 'Our rent is already far more than the shops on the next road are paying. How am I supposed to find that kind of money? If we put our prices up, the art students won't be able to afford to come here!' Ed bent over the table, suddenly looking exhausted. He put his head in his hands.

'Ed, go on up to the flat,' Zac said, noticing how tired he looked. 'Coco and I can finish up here.'

'Thanks, Zac.' Ed took his apron off slowly and fetched his keys from the kitchen. 'You're good kids. Zac, I'll see you up in the flat. Meantime, I'll be trying to invent a magic money-making machine.'

As Zac walked into the kitchen to put the last cups and bowls in the sink, he remembered standing there on a stool next to his mother, her hand gently resting on his back as she let him lick the bowl. Seven years since her death, the café was the only place where he could still really remember her. Here, the memories were so vivid, it was almost impossible to believe that she had gone.

He remembered sitting beside her, after the cafe was closed, with a jam jar full of rainbow-coloured pencils that she always kept especially sharp for him. He would draw new ideas for comic-themed food while she cashed up and Ed cleaned down the tables.

Zac washed the remaining dishes, thinking hard. There had to be something that he could do to help. The café was Ed's life's work. After Zac's mum had died, Ed had given up studying illustration to look after Zac, and with it, his chance of becoming an illustrator. Ed had put every penny that he had into keeping the café going for Zac. There was just no more.

Zac put the last plate on to the rack to dry and made a decision. 'I'm going to sell the comic,' he said as he reached the counter.

'What, our Salamander Smith comic?' Coco asked, looking up from the table that she was wiping. 'I don't think it's well known enough to make much money; we only sell about eight copies a month and I think the staff buy most of those to be kind.'

'Not Salamander.' Zac spoke slowly, '*The* comic!'

'Not *the* comic!' Coco gasped. 'Ed would never let you. He knows you'd give away every single other thing that you own in the world and then fight to the death for that comic.'

'If it's the comic or the café then I have to,' Zac said. 'I can't let Ed lose it. He needs this place. It's kept him together since Mum died.'

'But the *Komodo* first edition?' Coco pleaded. 'You love that comic. Your copy is the only one in the world. It's irreplaceable. Isn't there another way? Any other way?'

'Can you think of anything?' Zac replied.

Coco tried desperately. But her mind had frozen … nothing … just blank pages … 'Argh! Superheroes don't freeze like this. Where's my light bulb moment?! I need to think our way out of this!'

In silence, they stood up and walked together to the revolving door, and back into Cosmic. The bright colours and flashing lights that illuminated the shop in daytime were shades of grey in the evening gloom. The superheroes, now barely discernable, cast awkward shadows in the weak light of the street lamps. It was not hard to imagine armies of master villains crawling from their lairs, slipping out between the pages of the comics into the dark shop. Coco shuddered slightly as she walked through.

Cursing her over-active imagination, she moved fractionally closer to Zac's side. Shoulder to shoulder, they descended the five gallery steps. Their eyes adjusted slowly to the darkness as they approached the alarmed case at the very back.

Coco froze. Zac's keys clattered to the floor.

The case ... was empty!

KOMODO JONE

AND SAM WILSON IN...

THE CASE OF THE EMPTY VAULT

ISBN 978-1-909991-65-1
9 781909 991651

Despite Ed's frantic call, the police insisted that the theft was not an emergency. They said that as a non-urgent matter, they couldn't come around before morning to take fingerprints.

Alannah had been dropping Grace at a friend's for a sleepover when she heard the news via text from Emma. She arrived back at the shop laden with bags of chips and cokes for Zac and Coco and wine for the adults. They all sat on the shop floor, eating and drinking, while she tried to cheer everyone up with funny stories about the days of the band with Zac's mum and Emma.

Still in shock, neither Coco nor Zac could touch their chips. The stories swirled around their heads not reaching their ears. Zac had once positioned a battered red leather armchair at the perfect angle for viewing his special comic. He slumped into it now, in front of the empty case where his comic should have been, and stared.

Eventually, Ed and Emma gave up persuading Coco and Zac to go up to bed and dropped the kids' duvets downstairs, hugged them both and left to go up to their own beds.

The rest of the night was measured out in Coco's frantic pacing to and fro across the gallery as she tried to make sense of it all. Hour after hour passed by, her mind flooded with wild theories and scattered thoughts – until she too collapsed exhausted, curled up on a beanbag at Zac's side. Both of them finally closed their eyes, just as the sun was rising.

The arrival of the police just after nine a.m. jolted them awake. Emma and Ed talked to the officers while Coco helped Sasha to get the shop and café ready for opening. Handfuls of chocolate buttons regularly shovelled into her mouth, helped to keep her awake. She strained to catch snatches of Ed and Emma's conversation with the police as she worked. Coco left Zac in the gallery while she went next door, knowing he was still too stunned and upset to move. When she'd finished putting out the chairs and tables, desperate to keep busy, she went back into Cosmic. By now, Emma and Ed had taken the police into the cash office to talk privately.

'Hey, what's with the police cars outside?' Josh, one of their most regular customers, called across the shop. He'd ignored the 'Closed' sign, as he often did, and come straight in.

Zac looked around. 'The comic's gone,' he mumbled.

'Not *the* comic?' Josh went over to Zac. He loved the original *Komodo Jones* pencil draft almost as much as Zac and Coco. He lived in a flat on the top floor of the building – two floors up from Coco's, one up from Zac's. There weren't many days when he didn't drop by on his way in or out, just to admire the comic.

Zac nodded, glumly.

'When? And how?' Josh asked.

Coco was glad to share some of the thoughts that had been churning inside her head. 'Sometime yesterday after lunch and before six thirty when we locked up. I've been running over the timings all night.'

Zac took over. 'Emma said it was safely in its case when she was helping a customer at lunchtime. Then everyone was flat out with all the author-signing craziness. When we came in to look at it at about seven, after we'd closed up,' Zac said, 'it was gone.'

'I wonder how many customers passed through between lunchtime and the evening?' Coco said.

'An impossible number to track down,' said Zac.

'But the case is alarmed, isn't it?' Josh said. He walked over to examine it.

'Please don't touch it!' Coco said. 'I don't think

they've fingerprinted it yet.'

Josh dropped his hands to his sides. 'But the alarm didn't go off. I would have heard it, even if, by some miracle, you hadn't. I was in all afternoon yesterday.'

'And we were all working all day, and here in the evening too,' added Zac

'That's the thing that I just couldn't work out last night,' Coco said. 'Only Ed, Emma and Sasha know the code. It doesn't make any sense.'

'So what do the police think happened?' Josh finished examining the case and turned to face them.

'They don't know. I heard them tell Emma to keep an eye online in case someone tries to sell it,' Zac said.

'They've got no idea,' Coco whispered. 'I overheard one of them say that they had "better things to do than chase after some kid's joke book!"'

'How could anyone call one of the greatest works in comic history a *joke book*? It's unbelievable!' Zac shook his head.

'So, they don't know why the alarm didn't go off either?' Josh asked.

'Not yet, the locksmith who fitted it can't come until tomorrow,' Coco replied. 'When the police fingerprint the keypad, it might bring up something.' She didn't sound hopeful.

Josh checked his watch. 'I've got to go, but I'll be back as soon as I can. I just came by to grab my copy of the new *Komodo* and to give you this.' He handed Zac an article from a newspaper.

Zander Cooper, famously reclusive creator of superhero Komodo Jones, leaves his mountain hideout to make an appearance at this year's Comic-Con.

'Oh my God!' Coco said, reading over Zac's shoulder. 'That's incredible! No one has seen him for years.'

'Wow. Emma might get to meet him ...' Zac's voice lifted slightly for the first time.

'Is Emma going to Comic-Con this year?' asked Josh.

'Yes, she has to – I mean, she loves it too, but yes, there's always work stuff she has to do there,' babbled Coco.

'I wonder why Zander Cooper's surfacing now?' said Josh. 'He's always avoided public events and I heard he hasn't even met anyone from his publishers. He just does everything by post!'

'Who can guess?' Coco said. 'We're his biggest fans ever and we know everything that we can know about him ... which isn't a lot ... He's as much of a mystery as this disappearing comic!'

After saying goodbye to Josh, Coco returned to find Zac angrily hitting the buttons on the pinball machine.

'That comic is an important piece of art,' his voice cracked slightly and he looked down, 'and my only chance to save the café.' Zac pulled the sleeves of his hoody over his fists and pressed them against his eyes, hard. 'It was from Mum. Why won't the police take it seriously? A crime happened here. It's the stealing part that's wrong. Just because it's not a diamond ring, it doesn't make it less of a crime.'

Coco had never seen Zac look so angry. She perched on the arm of the chair next to him. 'We're going to work this out, Zac. With or without the police.' She sounded a lot more confident than she felt.

'I'm not so sure.' Zac spoke quietly, leaning on the machine. 'That comic could be on a plane to anywhere by now.'

'Well, we can't just give up!' Coco picked up the duvet and pillows from the chair. Zac's copy of the latest Komodo Jones fell to the floor. She reached down to grab it. 'Think about our heroes ... Komodo would never just give up.' Coco placed the comic down in front of him on the pinball machine. 'We need to be more like Komodo!'

Zac refused to look at her, or the comic. 'We're not in a comic story! This is my life and Ed's. And yours. Mr Haines is your landlord, too. He'll do the same to the rent on this shop too ... so it's a problem for all of us.' Zac pushed extra hard on the buttons of the pinball machine. 'What are we going to do? It's a disaster.' He kicked the machine. Its lights began to flash.

Trying to ignore him, Coco studied the cover of the new issue. Komodo took up the entire page. The slogan snaking across the bottom said, 'Let the truth win ... Let the adventure begin!' in bold green lettering.

'We can't change what *has* happened ...' Coco paused as the thought formed, 'but we can change what *is* going to happen. Come on, Zac! Open it and start reading,' she begged, tapping the comic with her finger so he had to look at it. 'We need all the sleuthing ideas we can get. We need to think like Komodo!'

Coco quietly stepped away, across the floor towards the latest edition display shelf 'Komodo wouldn't see the empty case as a disaster – she'd see it as a mystery: a case to be solved, a chance for a new adventure.' She turned to look at Zac again. 'We've got to change the way that we think about this. The rent rise and the theft – it's our opening scene. It's a beginning ...'

'Or it's the end of everything.' Zac stared over at the empty glass case once more.

'Zac, please! We've got to try,' Coco begged one last time. 'You were doing this for Ed, remember?'

Finally, Zac forced himself to look around him. He remembered his mum telling him that when she had first looked at the old dusty, dirty, damp café next door, before she had transformed it, she knew that, if you could just imagine it, almost anything was possible.

Then he noticed the comics that were on the display shelf where the latest editions were kept. Each comic had a bright slogan across it: 'Cracking case!' proclaimed one. 'Crime doesn't pay, but the criminals will!' stated another. 'Catch them while you can!' said the next one, 'Hero or zero?'

'Coco?' Zac turned back to face her.

'Yes,' Coco said.

'Did you do this?' Zac waved towards the comics.

Coco tried hard to look innocent, 'Do what?' she asked.

'Did you pick out all these titles, so that I'd be all, like, inspired?'

'Maybe ...' Coco said. 'Did it work?'

'Yes,' he said, a glimmer of hope in his eyes at last.

'Yay! Finally!' Coco tried not to leap up and down. 'We're going to find the comic and save the café! Help, I need my notebook!' She searched around frantically. 'I need to make lists: 'possible witnesses …suspects …motives …weapons …''

Raising a small smile, Zac found Coco's notebook under the beanbag. *'Weapons?'*

'Well, we can't rule anything out at this stage of the investigation,' Coco grinned, 'and I can't think without a proper breakfast.'

Armed with Coco's notebook and a colour-changing pen that Zac grabbed from the counter, they headed for the café kitchen.

CHAPTER FOUR

'The bacon has now reached my brain! I can think again!' Coco stood up with the rest of her bacon sandwich still in her hand. 'We need to start with the evidence!'

'Then we need to start gathering it right now. Before any vital clues get moved. Someone might be in the gallery at this very second, contaminating the crime scene!' Zac pushed his half-finished plate away. Coco followed him back to the gallery.

Hopping up on to a stool shaped like an alien dwarf, Coco grabbed on to the antlers of a space-moose's head with her left hand, so that she could look around the alarmed case. She'd loved the matching pair of space-moose heads so much when she had spotted them at a car boot sale a couple of years before that she had promised to give up cake for a week if Emma would buy them for her. She'd insisted that they hung them on either side of the precious comic, like guards.

Meanwhile, Zac carefully picked up and examined a row of superhero figures, replacing each one carefully in order. He swept his hand inside the coin pockets of the arcade machines and moved on to the low display table. He started underneath it and worked his way up and over, leafing through the comic books that lay on top.

'Find anything interesting?' Coco asked finally, extracting herself from the stuffing of the armchair where she had been looking for clues.

'Nope, just a load of junk,' Zac said, opening his hands to show her.

'Don't be so sure!' Coco said, throwing her own findings into one of the pillowcases to take up to the flat with them. 'Remember what Komodo says: "One person's rubbish is another's treasure". We just need to examine each piece and work out why it's here. Any one of them might hold the answer.'

Upstairs in Coco's flat, they sat down at the kitchen table and Zac spread out his findings. 'A dog biscuit, a licked raspberry bonbon covered in fluff, a key ring with some kind of logo and an appointment card for something or other. What about you?'

Coco stuck her head into the pillowcase. 'One pound twenty-seven, which I'm keeping,' She popped her head out and put the money on the table before disappearing back in again. 'A false fingernail – gross! Your favourite pen ...' She reappeared and rolled it over to him. 'That really good sharpener that I lost last year, a disposable camera, a notebook with lots of numbers written in, two unicorn hairclips and a pen lid.' Coco emptied the rest out on to Zac's pile, took out her notebook and started to list them all under EVIDENCE. She underlined it twice.

Zac put each item into an empty biscuit tin as Coco made a record of it in her notebook.

'Done!' Coco said as Zac put the lid on top. 'I wish that had biscuits in.' She got up and walked over to the cupboards, opening and closing them, in search of food. 'I'm still starving. Why is Mum always too busy to get any food in? If you and Ed didn't have the café next door, I would have starved to death years ago!'

'Coco, please, please, please can you just concentrate on this? We can get food later.'

'Sorry,' Coco closed the last cupboard, 'you're right.' Sitting down again, she grabbed the pen and notebook. 'So, where do we go next?'

Zac reached over, and wrote SUSPECTS at the top of the next clean page.

'How are we supposed to work out suspects?' Coco asked. 'It could have been anyone. If only we had put security cameras in when the glass safe was installed.'

'You can't put cameras everywhere. Anyway, people find a way around them or cover their faces. It wouldn't have helped.' Zac said.

'You're right,' Coco replied, 'and I don't want to be on film every time I dress up in the Batman suit when I think no one's looking.' Coco stared at the page in front of her. 'Right, let's start with all the people that we know were around that day and go from there ... Think.'

'Ed, Emma, Sasha, Alannah, Grace ...' Zac started.

'Grace!' Coco wrote her name down in capitals and went over it five times. 'I bet it's her. I told you she's a villain – it's written all over her!'

'But she'd only just arrived; she wouldn't have had time to plan it all out. Also, she couldn't be less interested in comics. What would she want it for?'

'The money, idiot!' Coco stared at him in disbelief.

'I hate the idea that whoever has it might only know how much money it will make, and not what it's really worth. What if they damage it?'

'They won't be able to sell it for as much if they do. Let's keep going with the list.' Coco stabbed at the page with her pen. 'Also, Grace is just evil. I bet it was her.'

'Josh was upstairs in his flat ... and, um, the

landlord? He was in the café – did he come to the shop yesterday, too?'

'Mum didn't mention it … but, maybe.'

'What about the regular customers? That woman with the red hair who always takes the latest edition out of its plastic cover to check it, then insists on buying an unopened one.'

'She's so annoying!' Coco said, adding her to the list. 'What about that precocious kid who thinks he knows more about comics than any of us in the shop?'

'Your mum said that the police would need to run the fingerprints from the glass case through their database once they'd taken them, to see if they match any known criminals. She didn't think we would know until next week.'

Zac sighed as he realised how little time they had to find the comic before they lost the café.

'I'm adding us to the list of suspects,' said Coco writing them down.

'Don't be crazy! We were together,' Zac said. 'So, unless you stole it when you went to get your notebook, I think we're in the clear!'

'Yes, true, but we don't know exactly when it was taken,' Coco said. 'Remember we didn't make it to the gallery section when we showed Grace around because she wasn't interested. We wouldn't have noticed whether it was still there or not because it's down the stairs! It could have gone earlier, *or* Grace took it when we left her alone. Argh! Why did I leave her alone?! Remember in *Komodo Jones and the Revenge of the Hawk from Hell*, it turned out that Komodo had taken the sacred eyeball from the pyramid herself, in her sleep, and had absolutely no memory of it. It was one of the hardest cases for her to crack!'

'Yeah, that was a tough one,' Zac said. 'But not relevant now. Please focus Coco ... yesterday was our busiest day ever, so I doubt we could list every customer that came in. We need to go back to the evidence and see if any of it suggests a possible suspect.' Zac took the lid back off the tin.

Coco took out the dog biscuit and sniffed, 'It doesn't smell suspicious.' She dropped it back into the tin.

Zac picked out the appointment card next. He turned it over in his hands to read both sides. 'Look at this!' Zac held the card right in front of her. 'The appointment on here is for twelve-thirty today in central London – that's half an hour from now. If we go straight away, we can find out whose appointment card this is.'

'At last, a lead!' Coco said, jumping up, 'Who's the

appointment with?'

'Alexa Marvella at the UCTA, 47 Tempest Road, SE1.' Zac read off the details.

'I've never heard of her,' Coco said. 'She's not one of our regular customers. Or, if she is, she's never ordered anything. Or at least not under her real name! Maybe it's a pseudonym! Oh my God, maybe she's a spy! A ninja assassin who needs the comic to –'

'*Coco!*'

'Huh?'

'You're going too fast! Let's stick to what we know, what we have. What do you think UCTA stands for?'

'No idea, but we're going to find out! Let's go.'

They both turned just as Alannah appeared in the doorway, laden with shopping bags.

'Hi you two,' she smiled, dropping the bags on the floor. 'I've got food. Shall I fix you some lunch?'

'Thanks, but we've got to go.' Zac stuffed the appointment card in his pocket. Coco tried not to look desperate with hunger as she threw the evidence back in the tin. Zac put the tin in his backpack and threw Coco's notebook in after it.

'Here, take these with you.' Alannah grinned and handed Coco a bag of apple custard doughnuts on her way out of the kitchen door.

Coco shot her a grateful smile, tucked the bag under her arm and ran down the stairs after Zac.

KOMODO JONES

AND SAM WILSON IN...

THE CASE OF THE FALLEN FILM STAR

ISBN 978-1-909991-65-1

9 781909 991651

The station was only five minute's walk away, four minutes at a jog. Coco and Zac made it in three, just in time to watch their train pull out.

'If you hadn't stopped for doughnuts, we would have made it!' Zac panted, as he bent over to catch his breath.

'Ca—an't ta—a—lk.' Coco collapsed on to a bench.

Checking the timetable and then his phone for directions, Zac planned out their route. 'There's another one in five minutes – the journey takes eleven minutes, the building is twelve minutes from the station. We might still get there just in time to catch the suspect leaving.'

'Sorry, Zac,' Coco wheezed. 'But it was doughnuts! Had any ideas about what UCTA stands for yet?'

'I'm not sure,' Zac said. 'It sounds familiar. Damn this old phone – the battery hardly lasts half an hour. Can I try yours?'

'You could,' Coco replied, 'but I've lost it, and I'm not allowed a new one until I "can be trusted with it". Coco imitated her mother's voice. 'Its only the third one that I've lost.'

'This year!' Zac laughed. 'Remind me not to let you look after the evidence!'

'She's so nice,' Coco suddenly declared as they waited for the train to pull into the station.

'Who?' said Zac, looking around.

'Alannah!'

'You're just saying that because she gave you doughnuts.'

'Yes, probably – but I do like her. So, what do you think UCTA stands for?'

'I still don't know. I guess we'll find out when we get there,' Zac said.

'It could be University of *something*?'

'Maybe ...'

'Or *something* Comics, *something*, *something*? Oh! Comic Trading?! Oh my God! A massive company that buys and sells old comics! That's why they wanted it! They sent a professional in and –' Coco said, pressing the open buttons on the train door repeatedly before they had lit up.

'Coco! What does Komodo say about this?' Zac asked her.

'About what?' Coco looked confused.

'Guessing! "Start with what you know, not what you think."'

'But we don't know anything! We *have* to guess!' Coco pressed harder.

'We know where the building is – be patient!'

'I can't be patient ... it takes too long!' Coco said as the doors finally opened.

'Are you going to share those doughnuts, at all?' Zac asked as they sat down and Coco took out her second one.

'Ah, yes, sorry, I meant to ... Here you go.' Coco passed the bag across. 'Sorry, there's only a squashed one left.'

A few minutes after leaving the train, they rounded the corner. The entrance to the giant office block was straight in front of them. They scanned the list of businesses on the sign outside until they saw the only one that matched the letters on the card – 'It's the United Comic Talent Agency.'

'Wow!' Coco tried not to jump up and down with excitement. 'This is it. We've cracked it. The suspect must be going there to sell the comic! We're going to find out who took it and they'll have the comic with them and we can get it back. Easy!'

'We don't know that the *company* sells comics – but maybe someone who works there does?' Zac said.

Coco paused. 'True. Let's go in and find the boss and get him or her to find out.'

'But what if the boss is involved? Or no one in the company is? I don't know what to do.' Zac stopped still.

'We have to go in!' Coco tugged his sleeve towards the building.

'Yes, but then what? We can't just jump out from behind a door and arrest them!'

'True.' Coco thought. 'Let's call the police now, so that they're ready when we catch them.'

'No way! The police didn't take any of it seriously at the shop. They're hardly going to be pleased if we call them and then it turns out we're wrong. I'm sure that you can get into serious trouble for wasting police time,' Zac said.

'We're not wasting their time,' Coco replied. 'It all makes perfect sense. The comic goes missing. We find an appointment card at the crime scene; it's for someone who sells comics – stolen comics, if we're right. In fact, we might have uncovered an entire crime ring in stolen comics. We could be heroes!'

'Yes, it's all going to be that easy!' Zac shook his head. 'And then there'll be a parade and we'll get a huge reward and actual superpowers!'

'I've got a plan,' Coco said. 'Trust me.'

'It'll need to be better than that last one, or we're in real trouble!' Zac grinned as they walked up the front steps.

Coco and Zac flowed into the building caught up in a stream of people. The giant structure seemed to be breathing people in and out at an alarming rate. Coco and Zac pushed themselves out through the herds of suited humans, narrowly avoiding injury from swinging briefcases.

They looked around an entrance hall the size of a church. There were eight sets of lifts behind waist-high metal barriers, three reception desks, two fully-grown trees and a sculpture of something that looked like an origami elephant. The ceiling was so high that you could have stored an aircraft in there.

'There are over twenty businesses working out of this building. We don't even know which floor we need and no one is going to let two kids past those barriers without finding out what we are up to!' Zac turned around and headed back towards the front door.

Coco grabbed his sleeve and pulled him with her. 'I told you, I've got a plan. Follow me.'

Reaching the largest of the reception desks, Coco picked out a receptionist who was on the phone, looking bored. 'Hi, my dad works here. I'm meeting him in the lobby, but I'm desperate for the toilet. Is there one that I can use please?'

The receptionist buzzed them through the barriers without looking up. 'Second floor, turn right out of the lift and head straight through the double doors at the end of the corridor.'

Once in the lift, Zac matched the name on the appointment card with the right floor. 'Right at the top – the fifteenth floor,' he said.

Coco pressed number two.

'What are you doing? I said fifteenth floor.'

'It's just that now that I'm thinking about it, I really do need the toilet,' Coco said.

'Right now?' Zac said as they stepped out on the second floor. 'When we're about to catch the person who took the comic. Really?'

'I'll be quick, I promise.' Coco looked at him

pleadingly before running out of the lift.

Zac followed her out and glanced anxiously at his watch: how long would the suspect be in the meeting? Five minutes, fifteen minutes, half an hour? They might have already missed the person on their way out. He pressed the lift button as soon as he saw Coco reappear.

'Run,' he called down the corridor. She reached the doors, just as they opened. The lift ascended to the fifteenth floor.

As the lift doors opened, Zac and Coco were momentarily stunned by the corridor of comic magnificence in front of them. 'Oh my God! They've got a 1954 original *Green Lantern* special.'

'And edition twenty-eight of *Aquaman!*' Zac practically stroked it with his eyes. 'There are only seven of those left in the world.'

'This is amazing, it's –'

They looked around at the sound of footsteps.

'*Josh!*' Coco and Zac gasped in unison as they saw him walking towards them.

Zac shook his head in disbelief. 'No, please not you!' he said.

'*How could you?*' Coco demanded, staring at him with her most fierce look.

Josh looked back at them in confusion 'What are you two doing here?'

'What are *you* doing here first?' Coco took a step towards him. It was less threatening than she had intended. Josh was sixteen and had reached his full height already. At barely thirteen, Coco was really short for her age and didn't quite reach the middle of his chest.

'I had a meeting ...' Josh said. 'I don't understand. Why are you here? And how could I do what?'

'Don't pretend that you don't know. We've got evidence: the appointment card! And you've got a motive! You love that comic – you come to visit it almost every day!' Coco stared straight at him.

'What are you talking about, Coco? I really don't understand.' Josh took a step sideways, away from her, straight into a pot plant. He caught it just before it hit the floor.

'See you soon, Josh,' a lady said as she walked past them. 'I look forward to you starting your work experience in the summer holidays.'

'Thanks so much. I'm really grateful for the opportunity,' Josh answered politely, before turning back to Coco and Zac. He looked so confused, so thrown, that they realised straight away they had made a big mistake.

'Work experience …?' Zac said. 'Sorry Josh … I think we might owe you an apology.'

Coco looked at her feet.

Back at The Comic Café, with a large planet pizza in front of them, Zac talked Josh through why they had thought it was him. They explained everything that they had worked out so far.

'Basically, our list of possible suspects is: everyone that came in the shop on Thursday – and everyone else,' Coco explained in between bites.

'We're waiting for the locksmith to come and look at the case tomorrow and for the police to get back to us about the fingerprints,' Zac finished.

'For the possible motives,' continued Coco, 'we've got: greed, financial desperation and random evilness.'

'I'm so sorry, Josh. We know you're not evil or desperate, or greedy,' Zac said. 'You were the last person we would suspect.'

'Well, I can see that's not true! I'm on your suspect list!' replied Josh.

'So are we!' pointed out Coco. 'We're just being thorough!'

'I know – it's okay. I can see how you thought the theft was connected to the appointment card. I wondered where that had gone. It was lucky that I'd put the meeting in my phone. But UCTA doesn't trade in comics, they just represent artists and writers,' Josh said. 'I could never take your comic. I love it, obviously, but I wouldn't want to have to hide it away from the rest of the world.'

'But what other motive can there be for taking it?' Coco asked.

'Jealousy: a private collector who wants it just for the sake of owning it,' Josh said. 'Makes it most likely that it's someone who really knows about comics and the comic world.'

Coco showed Josh the complete list of evidence with the appointment card at the top, in case he had any ideas that might help. He glanced down it. 'The strawberry bonbon was mine too, so you can cross that off.'

Coco switched her pen round and wrote 'Josh' in different coloured ink next to the appointment card and bonbon.

'Aren't you going to cross me off the suspect list?' he asked Coco.

'Everyone remains a suspect until the case is solved,'

Coco said, turning the pen back to the green nib. 'Remember *Komodo Jones and the Case of the Illegal Lizard Trade?* Issue number twenty-four!'

'"Once the mystery begins ..."' Zac and Josh both quoted together, '"every lead must be followed, everyone must be suspected and no one can be trusted, until justice is done."'

'Exactly!' Coco laughed.

'Talking of people who can't be trusted,' Josh said, 'did the landlord find Emma? He was in Cosmic last week asking for her, but she was out on a delivery.'

'I don't think so,' Coco said. 'Do you know what he wanted?'

'He didn't say exactly; it seemed urgent though. I wondered whether it was about the plans to turn our whole block into fancy new flats like that one on the other side of the road. Have you heard? They want to have expensive chain shops underneath. My parents have no idea what they'll do, if it happens. They'll both be out of a job and we'll all lose our homes.'

'Our homes, too?' Coco asked. 'I thought it was just the shops!'

'It's everything. All the shops, the flats above and the art school.'

'So that's why he's putting the rent up.' Zac joined

up the dots. 'He wants us out, so he can knock the whole lot down and have it all rebuilt!'

'Actually,' Josh continued, 'now that I come to think of it, he was asking about the comic when he was looking for Emma. He wanted to know why it was in a glass case and how much it was worth.'

'*What?*' Coco turned on him again. 'The landlord was in the gallery section, a few days before the comic goes missing, asking about the very comic that was stolen and you only remember it now?'

'I've been desperate to get this work experience placement,' Josh explained. 'It's all that I've been thinking about. I was rushing to get my portfolio ready for the interview last time we spoke. It's only now that I've had time to think it through.'

'Is there anything else that you can remember that might be important?' Zac asked. 'Anyone else that you saw when you were there?'

'I'm so sorry, no, nothing that I can think of.' Josh shook his head. 'But Mum said that there's a meeting about the shopping centre plans at the local hall tomorrow. She's going. Mr Haines will be there then.'

Coco scooped up her stuff. 'We have to be at that meeting. We need to find out what's going on.'

KOMODO JONE

AND SAM WILSON IN...

THE REVENGE OF THE HAWK FROM HELL

ISBN 978-1-909991-65-1

9 781909 991651

Tripping over a row of suitcases as she ran through the front door of Cosmic, Coco shouted for her mother. 'Mum? Mum! Have you heard about the meeting?'

'Coco, I've been telling you since you were two, not to shout on the shop floor. It's not nice for the customers.' Her mother came out from behind the counter and straightened up the suitcases.

'Oh! Are Alannah and Grace leaving?' Coco said, temporarily distracted by the suitcases and the possibility of getting her room back from Grace.

'No, they're not. They're very kindly staying on to help me out.' Emma patted her pockets for her keys. 'I'm leaving for Comic-Con today.'

'But you can't go now! Not when the comic is missing and the landlord is breathing down our necks.'

Her mother straightened up the bags. 'Coco, I'm sorry, but I already had to delay the trip to be here for the signing. I was hoping your dad would be back by now, but he's been held up again. I'm sorry, he will get back as soon as he can – and so will I. I can't wait any longer; I really need to go. I've got so many meetings booked in with suppliers. The taxi is due any minute. You do understand, don't you?'

'Yes …' muttered Coco.

'I promise I wouldn't go if I could avoid it. But Ed will be next door, Sasha is covering the shop and Alannah will help her. Grace has kindly offered to look after you. Please be good. I'll be back on Thursday.'

Coco looked at her mother desperately. 'Okay, I get the rest of it, honestly I do: I know you and dad would rather be here and I know you have to work, but please, please don't put Grace in charge of me!'

'You'll be OK, Coco; it's not for long.' Her mother patted her pockets. 'Help! Where have I put my passport this time?' She opened her suitcase and lifted out the clothes.

Coco cursed her father's job as a foreign journalist, yet again, and helped her mother to look through the second suitcase for her passport.

'You are so lucky.' Coco said, trying a different tack, 'I can't believe that Zander Cooper is going to be making his first public appearance in fourteen years and you won't take me and Zac with you.'

'We can't afford the flights, and you have to go back to school on Monday, remember? Half term doesn't go on for ever,' Emma said, distractedly. 'Where *is* that cab?'

Coco finally found the passport in her mother's washbag and handed it to her. 'You have to stay here, Mum! They're trying to destroy our block. Cosmic, the café and our homes will all be gone. I don't want to move. This is my home. It always has been.'

'Tickets?' Emma said to herself. She opened her bag again and pulled the tickets out. 'Check.'

'Why didn't you tell me that they were trying to get us out of the flat and the shop?' Coco picked up the tickets that her mum had just put down on the counter and handed them back to her.

'Because I didn't want you to worry.' Emma dropped the tickets in her bag and closed it.

'It's a bit late for that!' Coco tried to keep the anger from her voice. 'At least don't make it worse by putting Grace in charge of me. It's way too much power for her.'

'Don't be silly. Passport, tickets, wallet – I'm ready to go,' Emma said, picking up her suitcases. 'Grace said that she'd be delighted to look after you. I need to go; I'm really sorry. It's important. We'll talk about the block as soon as I get home.'

'We might not have a home for you to come back to if you go now.' Coco pleaded.

'Taxi's here.' Ed called from outside where he'd been talking to Zac.

Emma reached for the door handle. 'Love you, darling.' Her mother kissed her on the head.

She followed her mum out of the door, and saw her jump into the taxi. The three of them watched as the taxi sped away.

'You two are alright to make your own dinner, aren't you? I need to go and lie down for a while,' Ed said.

'Don't worry, I'll close up the café, too,' Zac said.

'Thank you, Zac.' Ed turned to go, 'When's school?'

'Not till Monday – don't worry, it's all in hand,' Zac reassured him.

Ed smiled weakly, walked through to the back of the café and on up the fire escape to their flat.

'Is he okay?' Coco asked.

'Honestly? I don't think so.' Zac looked worried. 'Since the landlord came in, he's been really down. I haven't seen him like this before, not even –'

He didn't need to finish that sentence. They both

knew that Zac was talking about his mother's death.

'He's exhausted ...' Zac finished.

Later, in need of somewhere quiet to talk, Zac and Coco collected the biscuit tin of evidence from under Zac's bed, climbed out of his window on to the balcony that criss-crossed the back of the blocks, and walked up the fire escape to their favourite spot on the roof of the building. They had been sneaking up here for years to look out across South London in one direction and over the changing industrial docklands and bright lights of the river in the other. It wasn't a smart area, although the new music arena had brought shiny developments closer and closer to them. The contrast of new next to old made their block look even rougher around the edges. But, however shabby it was, it was their home; it always had been. And they loved it.

All the different events fought for Zac and Coco's attention: the theft, the rent increase, the planned development, Comic-Con, Alannah and Grace arriving and – according to Coco – apparently never ever leaving.

Was everything just happening at once, or were all the mysteries connected?

Under the warm sun of the May evening, they pulled out the old rug and cushions that they kept hidden in a battered bin for emergencies and poured out the evidence.

Putting the appointment card, bonbon and their own bits and pieces to one side, Zac added a few more items to the pile.

'What are these?' Coco asked.

'More clues – or not: things from the Lost Property box in the café that have been found since the theft.'

'Oh! Good idea!' She nodded approvingly.

"Thank you. It's only next door, so they might have been left there around the time of the theft, if he or she was loitering in the café.'

'Or dropped after,' Coco added. 'So what have we got now …?'

They looked at what was left and updated the list in Coco's notebook.

A pair of left-handed scissors
A manky plaster
A key ring with some kind of logo on it
A false nail
A voice activated mini- robot recorder
A disposable camera
A notebook with lots of numbers written in
Two unicorn hairclips
A pen lid
Still waiting for:
Finger print information
locksmith to examine glass case

'This one should be easy enough,' said Zac, putting the disposable camera in his pocket. 'We'll take it to the chemist to get developed; we should get the prints back really quickly.'

A strange feeling ran through Coco. 'I don't know if we should. What if it belonged to some tourists or something? I wouldn't like a couple of strangers looking at photos I'd taken.'

Zac shrugged. 'What else can we do? We might be able to return the photos to their owner, but first we have to get them developed to see who they belong to.' He paused and picked up the voice-activated robot recorder. 'This is great! Why don't you sell these?'

Coco took it carefully from her friend. 'They're faulty,' she said. 'You have to practically shout before they begin to record. Shall we?' At Coco's touch of the Play button, the lights on its head began to flash. The robot's arms moved up and down and its head twisted round. It began to play the recording, '... but I hate them, Mum!' The words came out of the speaker in the middle of its body.

'*That's Grace!*' Coco whispered, leaning closer to the robot. 'I'd know her squealing, whiny, sucky-uppy voice, anywhere!'

Grace's voice carried on whining out of the robot,

'… you promised we'd be moving into a beautiful big house in a fancy area. If I'd known we were going to end up in this end-of-the-earth pit hole, with these awful people, I would have gone with Dad and the step-witch. How were you and Emma ever friends? They're all so weird …'

Coco looked up sharply from the notebook full of numbers that she had started examining, to listen more closely.

'Shhh Grace,' Alannah's voice sounded severe as it followed her daughter's whine out of the robot. 'We're lucky to have somewhere to stay. It won't be for long. I've told you, the new house is almost ready. We just have to wait for the builders to finish the swimming pool and the second conservatory, and then we can move in.'

Grace's reply was too muffled to hear properly. Silence followed.

'Well, that rules Grace and Alannah out of the theft,' Zac said, pressing the 'stop' button on the robot and putting it back in the tin.

'Does it?!' exclaimed Coco. 'But they're horrible!'

'That's not a crime, Coco,' Zac said.

'It should be! How dare they?!'

'There's no motive. They clearly don't need the

money, so that's greed and desperation out – and neither of them know anything about comics, so it's not jealousy. And they need somewhere to stay, so they wouldn't want to upset your mum.'

'Never mind that!' Coco was on her feet and pacing! 'How dare Grace be rude about us and our home, while Mum's putting them up and she's sleeping in *my bed. I hate her!* I'd like to feed her to Jabba the Hutt. I hope they finish that swimming pool soon so I can drown her in it! And I am *not* crossing Grace off the list of suspects.' Coco sat back down and picked up the notebook from the evidence pile again.

'We need some leads to follow, Coco,' Zac said, sorting through the other bits and pieces. 'Apart from the meeting about the shopping centre plans tomorrow, we don't have anything to go on. At least narrowing down the list of suspects would help.'

'She's staying on,' Coco replied firmly.

She held up two of the pieces of evidence, 'The logo on the notebook with the numbers matches the logo on the key ring. I've been trying to work out where I know that logo from, but I can't think.'

Zac looked at them both next to each other. 'You're right! We can look up the logo online and find out what it's for.'

'Not now though,' Coco begged, 'I'm even too tired to eat.'

'Wow,' Zac said, 'you must be exhausted! OK, I'll do it when I get back to the flat. I guess that's one thing about Ed being too tired to check on me, I'll have unmonitored screen time, right when I need it most.'

Zac put the stuff back into the tin while Coco put the rug and cushions away. They walked down the fire escape and back up the main stairs to Coco's flat together.

'Night,' Coco said sleepily. 'See you in the café for breakfast, first thing.'

'Your first thing or mine?' Zac asked, knowing that Coco usually sprang out of bed at 6.30 in the morning, raring to go.

'Yours,' Coco said, noticing how pale Zac looked as he turned to walk on up to his flat. She thought he could use the extra sleep. 'Good luck with the logo,' she called after him.

The flat was quiet when she got in. She climbed into the camp bed that she had been sleeping on in the sitting room, glad that Alannah and Grace were out. She drifted off to sleep, dreaming about chopping Grace's hair off.

KOMODO JONES

AND SAM WILSON IN...

THE CASE OF THE ILLEGAL LIZARD TRADE
PART ONE

ISBN 978-1-909991-65-1

9 781909 991651

CHAPTER SEVEN

MAIN SUSPECT: LANDLORD
WHY: STRONGEST MOTIVE

MOTIVE: TO GET THEM OUT
SO THAT THE SHOPPING
CENTRE CAN GO AHEAD

'Where are you going?' Grace accosted Coco as she headed for the front door next morning. Coco noticed that Alannah's bag and coat weren't in the hall, so she had obviously gone out already.

'Stuff to do,' Coco replied grabbing her jacket from the chair.

'Yeah, too right, you've got stuff to do.' Grace pointed to the kitchen. 'The washing up for a start!'

'It's not my turn,' Coco said, her hand on the door.

'If I say it's your turn, it's your turn.' Grace crossed her arms. 'Your mum put me in charge of you. So, now, *I* say it; *You* do it.'

'You know she didn't mean it like that.' Coco took a deep breath to stop herself from charging at Grace like a wild bull. Stay calm, Zac needs help. Stay calm, Zac needs help, she repeated over and over again in her head before looking Grace straight in the eye. 'I've got to go. Can we have this conversation later?'

Stepping in front of Coco to block her path, Grace barred the front door. 'No shorty, we can't. So trot back into the kitchen and get your grubby little paws into the sink. I'm sure they need cleaning anyway.' She patted Coco on the head.

Coco sucked back down the fire that burnt her throat. She tried one last time. 'I haven't even had breakfast, so it's just your stuff that needs doing. I have to go. I'm late.' Coco tried to move past her.

'Kitchen,' Grace said, grabbing Coco's shoulder and shoving her. 'Now!'

Remembering that Grace didn't know the layout of the flats as well as she did, Coco pretended to head for the kitchen. Stopping just short of it, she ran into her mum's bedroom, opened the window and climbed out on to the balcony fire escape. After running along to the end and down the stairs, she jumped the bottom three steps, swerved around the garden tables behind The Comic Café and ran in through the back door.

The sound of voices and the smell of warm chocolate and freshly baked croissants led her to Zac and Sasha at the counter.

'Morning!' Coco grabbed a croissant and picked up the mug of hot chocolate that Sasha had poured for her. She ripped off half the croissant in one go. 'This is what I would like to do to Grace. I feel like I've done six rounds with a killer zombie croc this morning!' She laughed it off so as not to bring Zac down, but inside she still felt shaky with fury at the way Grace had treated her. Coco had never felt so powerless in her life. She could feel that Grace was trying to provoke her, and that if Grace managed it, Coco would be the one that ended up in trouble. Grace was older and much more comfortable around adults.

'Bad morning?' Sasha smiled at her sympathetically. 'Poor you, having Grace staying. Her mother needs to teach her some manners. She was in here yesterday, showing off with some friends from her posh little private school.'

Coco forced a grin. 'Nothing I can't handle,' she said.

'OK,' Sasha replied, pouring Coco some more hot chocolate, 'but I'm around if you need me.' Sasha had known Coco and Zac since they were born. She'd started out babysitting for them when she was still at school. In her early twenties now, she was like a big sister to them, and she could see that Coco wasn't herself.

'So how come you're working in here? Has Ed got you to leave the shop and run the cafe?' Coco changed the subject.

'No, I'm still working for you, don't worry! Ed just needed a hand here, so I said I'd cover when I can – when I'm not at Cosmic.'

'You'll be running backwards and forwards between the two?

'Don't worry, I'll just use the doors!' laughed Sasha. 'I don't need to know how you do that secret door thing! I think I'm too big to use it anyway.'

'We were just talking about the landlord's plans,' said Zac. 'Apparently there was a letter ...'

'What letter?' Coco asked.

'They both got letters six months ago about the rent going up. Ed and Emma's lease is the only thing stopping the development, but if they can't pay the rent the landlord can kick them out,' Sasha replied. 'He's done it to almost all the other shops on the block.'

'Ed's known about this for that long?' Zac said,

fiddling with the key ring.

'I'm afraid so,' Sasha said. 'He didn't want you to worry. I probably shouldn't have told you either, but –'

'Let's get back to finding the comic,' Zac said. He didn't want to think about Ed keeping things from him. 'At least that's something practical we can try to do. I did come up with something with the logo search.' Zac handed Coco a piece of paper. 'It turns out it's the logo for International Securities, a safe and lock supplier,' Zac said.

'A notebook and key ring with the logo for a lock supplier … Hmmm … curiouser and stranger,' Coco replied. 'So the locksmith and the landlord leap to the top of the suspect list today. We'd better take these hot chocolates to go, and get to the hall for the meeting.'

'That landlord's a criminal whether he took the comic or not,' Sasha said, pouring their drinks into take-out cups. 'He's stealing everyone's homes from under them. He's crazy getting rid of the art school. They keep cutting the arts to make way for more business, but if they don't train any artists, illustrators and designers up, it won't be long before there won't be any decent stuff for anyone to buy because there won't be artists around to imagine it or design it or make it.'

Sasha was studying illustration part-time at the art school and working at the café and Cosmic to pay for her studies. If the shopping centre went ahead, she would be out of a job and having to find somewhere new to study.

'You two get to that meeting and give them hell! I wish I could go with you but I've got to keep this place going for Ed. Check in later and let me know how it goes.'

Zac switched the sign on the door to 'Open' as they left.

Turning left at the end of their road, they walked past the front of the art school. The students' projects lit up each of the windows like an advent calendar on Christmas Eve. Some of the sculptures flowed out of the windows and streaming banners striped the front of the building. An exhibition of golden painted metal masks on iron poles had been mounted on the roof. Coco and Zac passed masks of sorrow, hope, despair, pity, anger and loss. The masks rotated with the wind showing the opposite emotion on the other side.

I wish the wind could blow us some better moods, Zac thought, admiring the way the light hit the burnished metal.

They turned left again at the next corner, where the buildings on their side of the street became more decrepit. Looking at their block, Zac took in the broken fences, collapsing under the weight of thorny wild roses that cascaded towards the ground. Weeds wove their way up between pavement cracks and crept into the boarded up shops that lined the road: the newsagent where Zac and Coco had spent their first pocket money on penny sweets and chocolate, the mini-market where they had been sent for milk and bread the very first time that they had been allowed to walk to the shops by themselves without an adult, the fish and chip shop where they had bought supper every Friday when neither Ed nor Coco's parents had the energy left to cook. Each one had been a part of their lives and all of them were now boarded up. Even the graffiti had started to fade. Paint peeled and nails rusted all along the road.

Coco looked from one side of the road to the other. They couldn't have been more different. The shiny, gleaming, glass and steel apartment buildings that loomed up on the opposite side of the road cast long, sharp shadows over them. The largest of the new buildings reminded Coco of a giant dentist looming disapprovingly over their own crumbling block, which, reflected in its mirrored surfaces, resembled a set of decaying dentures.

For the first time, she saw their block through the eyes of the people in the shiny apartments. She suddenly understood why they might prefer a bright new building to look at, and almost gave up hope. But those people had no idea of the lives that were lived in the block, and the people who worked in the shops and studied at the art school. They didn't know about all the famous illustrators who had started out as students there, who'd bought the first comic that had inspired them to draw in Cosmic and celebrated their first day at college in the café, doodling on the table cloths and chatting to Ed. Maybe if she could get them to understand the people who lived there, that they had great lives even without much money or smart homes, maybe she'd be able to get them to support the fight for the block to stay.

Coco and Zac were so deep in their own thoughts that it was only as they reached the hall at the end of the road that they remembered the new information about the locksmith.

'He's coming this afternoon. If we run back after the meeting, we should get there in time to confront him.' Coco said as they found seats near the front of the hall.

'Isn't that him, over there?' Zac asked, 'I remember what he looks like from when he fitted the case last year. I'm sure that's him.'

Coco tried not to stare as she looked over. 'It is,' she whispered back to Zac. 'That's definitely him. What's he doing here?'

Before Zac could answer, the landlord strode on to the stage, eyes, shoes and cufflinks glinting. He began, 'Good morning and thank you all for coming.

'Today, you are lucky enough to see the plans for the beautiful new shopping centre, which I am sure you will all agree will smarten the area up immensely, bringing this last shabby block in line with the wonderful new buildings that I have constructed opposite.'

Coco looked around at the people who had come in after them. They were mainly residents from the new flats, dressed uniformly in neatly ironed, grey clothes. Over in one corner, students and professors from the art school were a riot of colour, piercings and unusual hairstyles. They stood out like a fairground in a graveyard.

She spotted Alannah near the back. 'That's kind,' thought Coco. 'She must have come here for Mum and Ed.' Not for the first time, she wondered how someone so nice ever managed to have such an evil child – maybe there had been a switch at the hospital? Maybe somewhere there was a terrifying demon couple wondering why they had a cute human child ...

The man that Zac had recognised as the locksmith stood up to speak, 'On behalf of all of the shopkeepers who have been given premises in the new retail units in the block, I would like to thank Mr Haines for his investment in improving the area.'

Another woman stood up 'What about the shops that haven't been offered spots inside the shopping centre? What are they supposed to do?'

'All shopkeepers will be able to apply for space within the building,' the landlord responded, 'but we do want to keep it smart, so we will have to be really choosy about who gets in. And, obviously, tenants will need to be able to afford the new rents that go with a premium new property.'

'What about our homes?' Coco recognised Josh's mother as she stood up to speak. She and Josh's dad had been cleaner and caretaker of the block for twenty years. 'This block is our home,' she continued. 'We can't afford the fancy new flats. Where are we supposed to live?'

'Rehousing is not my responsibility,' the landlord said. 'Business is business. I'm sure the local council will be able to help.'

'What's going to happen to the art school?' one of the students asked. 'Wouldn't investing money in renovating the block, saving the art school, and supporting the existing residents and shop owners make more sense for everybody?'

'We don't need art schools,' the landlord said simply. 'They don't make money.' He turned to his assistant. 'Right, enough questions. Next slide please.'

'No! That's not enough questions!' Coco leapt up, surprising even herself. Her anger at the injustice of it all had fired up the bubbling lava that had threatened to explode over Grace earlier that morning. It overflowed now in an unstoppable stream. 'You're a thief! You're stealing our homes and our shops and the art school and our friends who live here ... and ... and ... you stole Zac's comic! You stole it so we couldn't pay our rent, so you could kick us out. You didn't even want to sell it for the money; you just didn't want us to be able to!'

Zac pulled her down next to him. 'You can't just accuse him. We don't have any evidence.'

'But he's got a motive. Greed!' Coco snarl-whispered back. 'Look at him, pretending he's some kind of superhero saving the area when actually he's destroying everything that's good about it.'

The landlord stood completely still. Murmurs tiptoed around the audience. Everyone was looking at Coco and Zac.

'Ha … ha … ha,' the landlord suddenly burst out. 'Go home and play with your toys, children. This is adult business. There's real, grown-up work to be done here, saving the area from people like your families.' He pointed to the door. 'Off you go now. Run along.'

Zac started to leave his seat.

'We're not going anywhere,' Coco said, standing back up. 'This is a public meeting and we're allowed to be here, just like everyone else.'

Zac dropped back into his seat and put his head into his hands. He'd seen Coco like this before and he knew they weren't going anywhere. The art students, professors and residents of the old block all cheered for her.

Slightly purple in the face, the landlord shouted at his assistant to hurry up with the next slide. An image of their block now was replaced by an image of an enormous, shiny new building on the screen. The whole of Zac and Coco's life was wiped out in the click of a mouse.

'No one talks to me like that,' the landlord snarled at them, as they filed out past him at the end of the meeting. 'I didn't take your comic, but I'm glad it's gone. Thanks so much for letting me know. If that comic was the only way you could pay up and stay on, then it was the only thing standing in my way, and now it isn't. You'd better start packing.'

KOMODO JONES

AND SAM WILSON IN...

THE JUSTICE THRONE

ISBN 978-1-909991-65-1

9 781909 991651

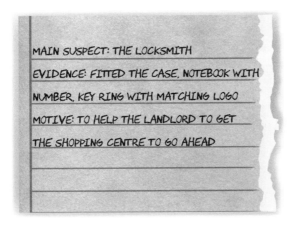

CHAPTER EIGHT

MAIN SUSPECT: THE LOCKSMITH

EVIDENCE: FITTED THE CASE, NOTEBOOK WITH

NUMBER, KEY RING WITH MATCHING LOGO

MOTIVE: TO HELP THE LANDLORD TO GET

THE SHOPPING CENTRE TO GO AHEAD

'Rats, rats, rats!' Coco paced up and down in the café kitchen. 'Now I've made everything worse!'

'You haven't,' Zac said, passing her a reassuring supernova flapjack from behind the counter. 'I wish I had the guts to stand up to people like that. It was really brave. Embarrassing, but brave.'

'It wasn't brave,' Coco took a half-hearted bite of flapjack and sat down. 'If I'd done it on purpose, it would have been brave, but I just couldn't stop myself and now the landlord knows that we can't pay the rent and I've made everything even worse. Not just for us, but for the whole block.'

'It *was* brave, Coco,' Zac repeated. 'There were lots of grown-ups there who didn't stand up for what they thought.'

'I think that we need adult help.' Coco nibbled around the edges, 'Maybe Grace and the landlord are right. We are still kids – maybe we can't do this on our own. We're dealing with millionaire business people. Who are we with our comics and big ideas?'

'Don't start believing that we matter less because we have less money. Being poorer doesn't make us less human. And who are we going to get to help us, anyway?' Zac asked. 'All the grown-ups that we know are on our list of suspects. Josh has told us everything he can remember, Sasha is flat out with the shop, Ed is, well, he's so tired; he's just working and sleeping, and I think he's in shock. And your parents are both away.'

'I just don't know what to do next,' Coco said.

'Komodo wouldn't ask Superman for help, would she?' Zac said, putting a plate of tuna melts (cheesy sharks) down in front of her. 'Table number sixteen, please.'

'Obviously not!' Coco hopped off her stool at the counter and grabbed the plate. 'Komodo and Superman come from completely different universes. You know that! It would be impossible,' she said, walking out into the café to deliver the food.

'That's not what I mean,' Zac said when she got back. 'I mean she wouldn't wait to be saved by someone else. She'd be brave. She'd look at the evidence, think it through and keep going until she solved it. You're the one who keeps telling me that we need to be more like her.'

Zac glanced at his watch. 'The locksmith is due any minute, if he's finished sucking up to the landlord.' He took a plate of man on the moon (cheese) toasties over to table nine. Sasha called Coco to serve black hole doughnuts and monolith muffins to table twelve.

'Cheers, Coco,' Sasha called into the kitchen, as she and Zac headed for their door. 'Are you coming back afterwards? I could do with a hand.'

'I can't,' Coco apologised. 'I promised I'd go and help Alannah. She's not sure where all the new deliveries go, so I said I'd go and put the stock out.'

Checking behind him, Zac pulled the droid forwards. The door into Cosmic swung around.

'How does that thing work?' Grace's voice attacked them before the door had even clicked in place.

'Nothing you need to worry about,' Zac said, turning to face her.

'I'm not "worried" about it,' Grace answered. 'I just want to know.'

'Sorry, we can't tell you,' Zac said.

'Well, we could,' Coco said, 'but then we'd have to kill you.'

'Good to see that you still haven't had time to grow up since this morning, Coco,' Grace sneered. 'Were you too busy playing hide and seek all by yourself? Sorry that I couldn't come and find you, but I had better things to do. Don't worry, I've left you the washing up, and you can do my laundry too. Don't wreck anything.'

Grace threw a smile at Zac and sloped off. He raised his eyebrows at Coco, 'Wow, he said, 'she's not getting any less evil, is she? Are you OK?'

'Fine,' Coco said, 'but *she* won't be soon. I keep dreaming about ways to get her back, like hanging her over the side of the block by her ears until they stretch out and she has to live with giant ears for the rest of her life. Or shaving her hair off in the night and dyeing her scalp orange. If I have to live with her much longer, I'm going to carry them all out.'

Alannah was at the alarmed case with the locksmith when they entered the gallery. 'Nothing wrong with it at all,' he said, 'It's working perfectly. Whoever got in there knew the code. There's no two ways about it.'

'Oh well, that rules me out,' Alannah laughed.

'Are you absolutely sure that no one has broken into it?' Zac asked the locksmith. 'Only Emma, Ed, Sasha, Coco and I know the code. They're all like family. None of them would have taken it.'

'I'm a million per cent sure,' the locksmith said, peeling his gloves off.

'But why should we trust what you say?' Coco said. 'You're in with the landlord, and you get to benefit from the shopping centre and we found evidence linking you to the theft here, in the gallery section. Show him, Zac.'

Zac took out the key ring and notebook. 'They're yours, aren't they?' he said.

'We looked up the logo,' Coco added. 'It's a match.'

'What are all those numbers in the notebook?' Zac asked.

Coco jumped in before the locksmith could reply, 'I bet they're override codes, like in Komodo Jones and the Case of the Empty Vault.'

'Komodo couldn't work out how to solve the case until she discovered that there was an override code for the entrance to the vault and the person who had fitted it knew it and used it to break in,' Zac explained. 'You could have got into the case with an override code.'

'Yeah!' Coco agreed. 'Did you keep copies of our keys when you put the locks in? How long have you been planning this for?'

'Hang on a second!' The locksmith was furious. 'I came round here as a favour to your mum, to help you out – and you two stand there accusing me. You haven't even let me answer. I've had my locksmith business here on this street since before you were even born. Do you think that I could have built up the reputation that I have if I was keeping illegal copies of keys and using override codes?'

'Well, what are all those numbers then?' Coco asked, a little less sure of herself now.

'I'm a trainspotter,' the locksmith replied. 'They're all train numbers and times and locations – you can go and look them up if you don't believe me. And I can prove that I didn't take the comic because I was working at the time that your mum said that it went missing and my security cameras will show that I was in my shop.'

Taking his phone from his pocket, the locksmith swiped the screen, typed in the date and time of the theft and turned the phone towards them. They watched him talking to customers behind the counter. 'This is what you could have done with here: absolute latest, remote access security system. You'd have seen exactly who took it.'

'Not that useful now though,' said Zac.

'How do you explain the key ring?' Coco said as the

locksmith put his phone away.

'Every time anyone has a set of keys cut, I put them on one of those key rings. They're free from the manufacturers. It could have come off anyone's keys. Has someone here had new keys cut recently?'

'I don't think so.' Zac replied. 'Is it possible that *someone* could have used an override code?' he asked.

The locksmith paused for a moment – he could see how upset the kids were. 'The manufacturers keep them encrypted and only the owner of the case would be able to access them, but only after they'd gone through rigorous security checks to establish that they are the owner. Give them a call if you don't believe me.'

'So, no one except Emma could have got the override code?' Zac checked again.

'Absolutely no way. Whoever took the comic knew the code, or knew one of you well enough to guess it. Twenty years I've been in the business and no one has ever got into one of these. No difference here. Not a single sign of an attempted break in, and I've seen them all, drills, nail files, screwdrivers, hammers, fire extinguishers. If I were you, I'd forget override codes and start looking at the people who knew the code, or the people who know you all well enough to work it out. Most people don't make their codes nearly complicated enough!'

KOMODO JONES

AND SAM WILSON IN...

MIRROR MADNESS

ISBN 978-1-909991-65-1

CHAPTER NINE

MAIN SUSPECTS: ED, EMMA
AND SASHA
EVIDENCE: KNEW THE CODE
MOTIVE: FINANCIAL
DESPERATION

Between all the jobs that needed to be done for the comic shop and café, Coco and Zac didn't have a second to get back to the investigation until late the next morning.

'It has to be our parents – doesn't it?' Zac said as he opened the front door to his flat to let her in. 'I couldn't sleep all night thinking about it. It's the only thing that makes sense.'

'It doesn't make *any* sense. They would never take it without talking to you about it. Never,' Coco said, following Zac into the spare room that Ed used as an office.

'They might have, if they thought that I wouldn't let them have it. I would have, obviously.'

Zac carefully moved piles of paperwork and large artists' sketchbooks full of Ed's work from the chairs, so that they could sit down.

Glancing around at all the charcoal drawings stuck to the walls in random spots, Coco remembered that Ed had been studying art before Zac's mum had become ill. She walked over to take a closer look. 'God, he's brilliant, isn't he? I'd forgotten that Ed was at art school with our mums.'

'And Alannah,' Zac reminded her. 'Yeah, he's amazing. I wish I could find a way to help him to go back and finish his degree. I still feel bad that he gave it up to look after me and the café.'

'He loves you, and the café,' Coco said, walking back to leaf through some of the illustrations that Zac had moved to the desk. 'Look at this one, it's of your mum.'

'He still draws Mum a lot. I think it helps when he's missing her.' Zac joined her and pulled out the sketchbook underneath. 'Look, this one is full of them.'

Coco flicked through it while Zac switched on the computer. 'This feels really wrong,' he said. 'I don't like snooping around.'

'We don't have any choice; we have to find out

what's happened to the comic.' Coco closed the book and joined him by the computer.

Zac switched it on and they waited quietly as the old machine woke itself up.

Zac knew that Ed didn't have any passwords on any of his computer files because he had spent ages trying to convince him to be more careful. But he'd never managed it. Ed always replied that he had nothing to hide and nothing worth stealing. 'These people who steal things, they know the price of everything and the value of nothing,' was one of his favourite sayings, along with, 'Kindness, friendship, laughter and good food are all the riches that I need.' But that had been before the landlord had doubled the rent. The café and comic shop were good, busy, very popular places, but no small independent business could afford the amount of rent that the landlord was asking, and the landlord knew it.

The last internet search came up on the screen. It was a search for the value of the stolen comic.

'When was it? When did he look this up?' Zac slumped in his seat.

Coco checked the date next to the search history. 'It was … ten days ago. He doesn't use the internet much, does he?'

'He must have been considering this for ages,' Zac said, 'and then decided to take it after the landlord came into the café, when it was all suddenly so urgent and real.'

'So, what are you saying? That after the landlord came that day, Ed went out of the back door of the café, and then in through the back door of Cosmic?' Coco asked.

'Ed and your parents are the only ones with keys to the back door of The Comic Shop,' Zac said, nodding. 'They can't get any more cut now, because the lock's gone a bit weird and only the old keys will work.'

'And Mum's at Comic-Con now. They must know that they would get so much more for it with Zander Cooper actually there this year.'

'I'm afraid it all makes sense,' Zac agreed. 'Means, motive and the opportunity! Our parents know everyone in the comic world, so they can sell it. That's why they weren't panicking about the block, because they had a plan for the rent.' He paused. 'But then why *steal* it from me? From us?' he continued. 'That bit doesn't make any sense. I would have given it to him in a second. Not that anything makes any sense if Ed has stolen it, and lied to my face.'

'But if they've taken it so my mum can sell it at Comic-Con, the café and block will be saved and everything will be OK again. And we can stop hunting and life will go back to normal!'

'I've just said, it's never going to be normal again, knowing that Ed could steal from me.' Zac said. 'Why didn't he just ask?'

'Maybe there wasn't time,' Coco said. 'Click on to Comic-Con news; there might be something there about Zander Cooper.'

'The least they could have done is taken us along,' Zac said. 'I can't believe that Zander Cooper is going to be there. Thirteen years living as a recluse up a mountain in Vermont with almost no contact with the outside world except to send his manuscripts to his publishers, and now suddenly he's making an appearance at the biggest Comic convention in the world. Why now?'

Images of Zander Cooper being mobbed by fans flashed up. He looked drawn and nervous. 'He hates being surrounded by people. I wonder why he agreed to make an appearance this year. Maybe it's because of the film coming out,' Coco said. One of his other creations –*Land Dragon* – had just been turned into an epic movie. It was premiering at Comic-Con.

'Look, they're even reporting what Zander had for lunch,' Zac said, scanning through the social media feed. 'The sale of the original hand-drawn *Komodo*

Jones comic would be all over the internet.'

Headline after headline flashed up about Zander Cooper but nothing about the sale of the comic.

'There's not a word about it at all,' Coco said after a while. 'They're clearly not out there selling it.'

'They could easily have lined up a private buyer before they went,' said Zac. 'They know all the dealers and all the collectors. You're right, though, they wouldn't need to go to do that. So why? What are we missing?'

'I don't know. But, I do know that we need to keep looking until we find something,' Coco said. 'You keep checking through the emails and I'll look through all these papers.'

After half an hour of hunting and finding nothing much except bills and threatening letters from the landlord, they were both at a dead end.

'We need a food break,' Coco said. 'Luckily, I've got biscuits. It's not as bad as I thought having Alannah looking after us, apart from the Grace bit. At least Alannah keeps food in and Grace eats like a grasshopper, so all the good stuff is still in the cupboards!'

Zac sat on the floor next to her and took a biscuit

from the packet. He ate in silence but his brain was shouting one thought at him over and over again. 'Why had Ed lied?'

'What's in the safe over there, under that pile of laundry?' Coco asked, as she reached for her fifth biscuit. She lifted up the laundry and balanced it on top of a pile of boxes on a chair.

'It's where he keeps documents and passports and the cash from the café when he can't get to the bank to pay it in,' Zac said.

'There might be something in there that will help explain things. Do you know the code?' Coco asked, pressing all the buttons on the keypad.

'No,' Zac said, 'but knowing Ed, I could probably guess it. Try my date of birth.'

Coco tried the four digits. 'Nope ... Next?'

'Umm, my mum's birthday ... 2407.'

'Got it!' Coco yelped. 'We're in!' She opened the door and looked inside. There were paying-in books, chequebooks and lease documents. In a separate file at the bottom was a large envelope marked 'Kim'.

Coco handed it to Zac. 'I'll look through the banking stuff, you look through that.'

Zac glanced at the writing, 'I don't want to look

through it. It's stuff about Mum.'

'OK.' Coco took it back from him. 'You do the banking stuff and *I'll* do the envelope.'

ART SCHOOL GIRL BAND, POP POW, HAS BOOM AND SPLIT AT THE HEIGHT OF FAME!

After less than two years together, one huge hit and a number one album, Pop Pow has decided to split. Emma and Kim are both pregnant. They have decided not to bring their children up in the spotlight. After retiring from the pop world, they plan to open a comic shop and space-themed café, just around the corner from the art school where they all met.

Alannah, the third band member and mother of three year old, Grace,

made this statement: 'I want to show that you can be a mother and be famous too. I can't see what possible harm it could do to a child to have a rich and famous parent, so I will be continuing with my own solo career as Alannah Adonna, without the rest of Pop Pow.'

r

'It's funny how Mum never really talked about the band,' Coco said. 'This makes it sound like Alannah and our mums fell out over the split.'

Zac took the article. 'I don't know much about pop, but it doesn't seem as though Alannah's solo career went very far either.'

'Thank God our mums didn't carry on with it after they had us. I'd hate to have a famous parent,' Coco said.

'I know,' Zac agreed. 'Imagine being followed everywhere you go by bodyguards, and having newspapers taking your photograph and having an opinion every time you trip up or stay still.'

'Yeah!' Coco took the article back. She started to imagine life if the band hadn't split and shuddered. 'I can see the headlines now: "DAUGHTER OF POP SENSATION FALLS FLAT ON HER FACE IN A PUDDLE AGAIN – COULD IT BE PROBLEMS AT HOME? POP PRINCESS DAUGHTER WEES IN STREET."' She flicked through a few more pages of the file. 'Or "SCRUFFY DAUGHTER OF STUNNING POP LEGEND BRINGS SHAME ON THE FAMILY BY BEING SHORT AND CLUMSY."'

Coco put the article down into her checked pile and picked up the next piece of paper. She read the top line, hesitated, then handed it to Zac face down. 'Zac, it's your birth certificate.'

Coco knew that Zac had never been interested in who his real dad was. He'd been too young before his mum had died to understand anything, except that Ed had always been there for him. Ed picked him up from school and looked after him if his mum was busy at the café. Ed had cared for him and the café and his mum when she became ill. There hadn't been much room in all of that to wonder too much about a man who had left before Zac had even been born.

Zac held the piece of paper without looking at it. Less than a week ago, his life had plodded along: the pain of waking up every morning to realise afresh each day that his mother wasn't coming back had finally begun to recede, and he and Ed managed to put one foot in front of the other together.

He wasn't sure that he wanted any more surprises at the moment. The rent, the missing comic, the possibility of losing his home and the café, the possibility that Ed had stolen from him – that seemed to be enough for one week.

But something in him couldn't stop his eyes from scanning down to the space under 'Name of Father.'

'Zander Cooper ...' he read slowly.

'Zander Cooper, what?' Coco asked, wondering why Zac was saying the name of their comic-creator hero.

'Zander Cooper,' Zac said again, looking completely confused. 'Zander Cooper?'

'Why do you keep saying Zander Cooper?' Coco said, snatching the birth certificate from him. 'Are you trying to wind me up?'

'Zander Cooper.' Coco read from the birth certificate. 'Zander Cooper, Zander Cooper, Zander Cooper. Oh My God! Your dad is *Zander Cooper!*

Coco leapt up and started jumping up and down.

'Your real dad is Zander Cooper – the one and only Zander Cooper – the creator of the best comic character in the entire world. Oh my God. Your real dad made *Komodo Jones*! I'm going to die right now of shock.' Coco fake-fainted on to the floor with her legs in the air, clutching Zac's birth certificate against her chest.

Zac still hadn't moved.

Coco got bored waiting for him to laugh at her, and sat up. 'This is huge. God, I'm so jealous, I wish my dad was Zander Cooper. He's the most famous person in comic history.'

'You just said that you'd hate to have a famous parent,' Zac said, shaking his head, trying to force the information to find a place in his brain where it made some sense. He couldn't. 'Anyway, it could be a different Zander Cooper,' Zac said, 'just someone with the same name.'

'Don't be ridiculous! What are the chances of that? It's hardly a common name. Look, his middle name is Isaac.' Coco pointed to the piece of paper. 'That is your full name. You must be named after him.'

'But my surname is Johan not Cooper,' Zac said, trying to rewire his entire existence and everything that he thought he knew.

'So your mum gave you her surname. It happens,' said Coco.

She started jumping up and down again. 'That's it! I've got it! Mum had to go to Comic-Con. She hasn't gone to sell the comic; she's gone to warn Zander Cooper, *your biological dad*, that the comic has been stolen.'

'Why would Zander Cooper care if the comic was stolen?' Zac asked. 'Why would he care about me at all? Or any of us? He left, a long time ago.'

'I don't know,' Coco said. 'I just can't think of any other reason. Anyway, what's important is that Ed didn't steal the comic!'

'We still don't know that. And he knew who my real father was and he didn't tell me,' Zac said. 'That's lying and it's as bad as stealing.'

'It's not. It isn't! Sometimes it is …' Coco said. 'But you never asked who your biological dad was. You always told me you didn't care. And sometimes people have to hide the truth. We lied to get into see the comic trader – if we hadn't done that, we might not have seen Josh, who told us about the landlord, who led us to the locksmith, who pointed us in this direction. And then we'd never have found out that your real dad is Zander Cooper …'

'You're probably right. There's just … too many thoughts …' Zac said. 'I feel like I've been flipped upside down and inside out. Shall I tell Ed that I know? And that I found out by looking through his stuff? That I thought he was the thief? That he still might be? Too much!'

Coco stopped jumping and started to pace. 'Let's go back to the first question: why would Zander care if the comic was stolen?'

'There's an even bigger question,' said Zac. 'How did he know our mums? He lives in America.'

Coco hadn't thought of that. 'And why haven't they even mentioned knowing him? I mean, it's one thing not to admit they had a relationship. But they could have admitted at least knowing him.'

Zac nodded. 'Especially since we're the biggest fans of Komodo Jones ever. What a coincidence, hey?'

'It's not a coincidence,' said Coco. 'It's fate. The Universe has spoken!'

'Shame Zander Cooper didn't want to tell the world that he had a son,' Zac said, sadly. 'He clearly didn't want anyone to know.'

Coco started to pace. 'Zac! That's it. That's why the comic has been stolen.'

Zac looked up. 'Why? I don't get you.'

'What if there's a link to you in there? Someone could use the comic to sell the story to the papers or to bribe your dad.' Coco stopped to think. 'Remember *Komodo Jones and the Case of the Fallen Film Star?* She couldn't work out the motive, even though she had a clear suspect and all the evidence. Then it turned out that there was a secret message hidden in the map that had gone missing and they needed it as a bribe.'

Coco stopped for a minute to let it all sink in. 'If whoever took it knew that it linked Zander to you, they'd get more money from selling the story about your real dad than just from the comic,' Coco said. 'Especially with him making a public appearance after thirteen years in hiding.'

'I've read all the same *Komodo* stories that you have, you don't have to keep reciting them to me,' Zac snapped. 'And he is *not* my real dad. Zander Cooper is just my biological dad. And I don't care if they bribe him, or sell his story. He left. He deserves whatever happens. Ed's my real dad, at least he was – he might not have stolen from me, but he still lied to me.' Zac shook his head disbelievingly. It was the thing that made the least sense to him. He threw the birth certificate down and walked out.

KOMODO JONES

THE RISE AND FALL OF KOMODO JONES

ISBN 978-1-909991-65-1

Coco followed Zac into the kitchen. 'What did we miss in the comic?' she asked him again. 'We know the story in the original version that you owned wasn't the same as the one that got published. Maybe it was different for a reason.'

'Sorry,' Zac said, pouring himself a glass of water. 'I know that you are just trying to help, but I don't want to think about it.'

Coco pulled out the chair next to her and Zac sat down. 'We can't avoid the truth, Zac, even if you don't like it. It's still there. Zander Cooper is your father and we need to work out the missing link. We still need to save the block. What's in the comic? Think!'

'It's ages since I read it, because it's been in that case since last year. I know the main parts of the story, and I remember Mum always telling me to look after it and never to lose it.' Zac scratched his nail along a groove in the kitchen table.

'I've only read it once because you wouldn't let

anyone touch it,' Coco said. 'Even then, you insisted on turning the pages for me.'

'You would have got jam on it,' Zac said, still trying to remember the story line. 'It's a different version of Komodo's origin story...'

'Yes, everyone knows that. We need the rest, the detail, the hidden parts,' Coco said.

Zac carried on trying to remember. ' In this version, there's no Sam, and Komodo is older, and she has a family. She invents the truth serum herself, she has to rescue her baby son from a Komodo dragon at the zoo. That's when she realises that she can talk to amphibians. Then her husband leaves because the villains are after him, to get to her. They're trying to frame him. He was going to end up in jail. So ... he goes to live in hiding up a mountain ...'

'Just like the real Zander Cooper!' Coco said. 'That's the link. It's his story too.'

'It doesn't seem like much of a link to me. I'm pretty sure my biological dad didn't leave to escape jail, or because mum had super powers,' Zac said.

'You don't know why your dad left,' Coco said. 'You didn't know who he was until ten minutes ago!'

'I'm still pretty sure it wasn't because mum was an amphibian- communicating trainee lawyer who beats up gangsters after college!' Zac said. He had picked up his birth certificate again and was tracing his finger over the letters spelling out his father's name.

'Did he leave without a trace in the story?' Coco asked. 'Or did he leave Komodo some way to contact him? You have to think, Zac!' Coco said. 'What if she had needed him?'

'I am thinking.' Zac stared out of the window and tried to turn the pages of his beloved comic in his mind. It hurt to think about it, but he forced himself to try to remember every word and picture. '... That's it! There was a phone number! Komodo's husband gives her a phone number in case she or their son is ever in real danger. I remember the drawing, because I always had a stupid urge to dial it when I was younger, to see what happened.'

'Then Ed and Mum would have known that it was there. They would know that if the comic got into the wrong hands, someone could tap Zander Cooper's phone to prove that he has a son,' Coco said. 'Maybe that's the real reason they put it in an alarmed case. Maybe they've just taken it to hide it better? If we can find the number, we can just dial it and warn him ourselves!'

'But, if Ed knew there was a secret phone number, if he really needed it, he would have just opened the case, written it down, and replaced the comic – he definitely wouldn't have risked losing it, or taking away my chance to talk to Zander Cooper, would he? I know I've doubted him recently, but I know he would never do that,' Zac said. He felt some relief as he realised this definitely ruled Ed out as a suspect. 'The number has gone with whoever stole the comic!'

'Damn it!' Coco said jumping up and starting to pace. 'I need more biscuits.' She grabbed an open packet from the counter and stuffed one into her mouth.

'It's no good. I can't picture it. All I remember is that it started with a zero,' Zac said as Coco came back in, 'and then maybe a two, or a five. I'm trying to remember how it looked on the page … Argh! I read it so many times!'

'What was it written on when he gave it to her in the comic?' Coco spluttered crumbs everywhere as she paced. 'Was it a notebook, or a scrap of paper, or …'

'Chew! We will work this out,' Zac said, looking up at her. 'You've got time to eat and talk.'

'Sorry, I got a bit carried away. It just feels like the answer is so close.' Coco was still spitting crumbs as she spoke.

'I think it's coming back to me,' Zac said. 'Page one … Komodo chasing villains, page two … they see her going back to her husband, page three ...'

Suddenly, the doorbell buzzed loudly.

'Noooo!' Zac banged his hand on the table. His thought chain was interrupted, just as he had turned the pages of his memory to the crucial scene in the missing comic.

'I'll get it.' Coco walked to the door, and opened it. 'Hi Alannah, is everything OK? Do you need help locking up the shop?' She realised that it must be closing time.

'Thank you so much for offering, but it's all done,' said Alannah. 'Sorry to disturb you both, but I just wanted to ask if you know why there might be money missing from the till? I've just done the cashing up and there's fifty pounds missing. I just wanted to check that neither of you had borrowed it.'

'Nope, Zac and I have been up here all afternoon,' Coco said. 'Mum sometimes thinks there's money missing and then it turns out that she just miscounted. It's easy to do. Zac and I can recount it for you, if you like.'

Alannah shook her head. 'No, it's not that. I've double-checked it.' Alannah looked hesitant. 'It's just that if you didn't take it, we need to find the person who did ... and I hate to have to tell you this, but

Grace says she saw Sasha by the till this afternoon. I can hardly bear to consider it, knowing how close you all are, but Grace thinks she might have taken it. I didn't think that she was capable of stealing from you but if she can take your parents' hard earned money, what else could she have taken?'

Alannah paused and put her hand on Coco's arm before finishing. 'Anyway, I just thought that you ought to know, with the comic missing and everything.'

KOMODO JONE

AND SAM WILSON IN...

THE SILENT SCREAM

ISBN 978-1-909991-65-1
9 781909 991651

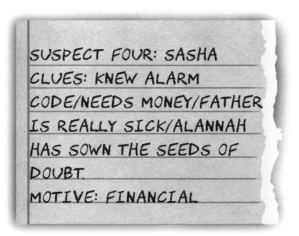

'Do you think Sasha could have taken it?' Coco asked Zac as Alannah left.

'Well, if Ed is capable of lying to me, then anyone is capable of anything.' Zac said. 'And if anyone had to take it, I would rather that it was Sasha. I know that she needs the money desperately to look after her father. I just don't think she could ever steal.'

'You're right. Sasha would only take it if there was no other choice in the world.' Coco said. 'Same as if she took the till money.'

'Can we get out for a while?' Zac asked. 'I need to sort my head out and I can't do it here. And I don't really want to talk to Ed yet'

'Sure,' Coco said, 'The roof or the river?'

The mismatched assortment of buildings that they walked past towards the Thames resembled the jumble inside Zac's head. Disused power stations huddled in amongst churches, apartment blocks, building sites, housing estates, museums and shopping arcades. Brand new high-rises forced themselves up between low-rises, confused and unintegrated.

Coco and Zac walked without talking, both of them knowing which direction they were going, as if on autopilot.

Heading down the steps, into the long pedestrian tunnel that ran under the river, Coco spotted Sasha ahead of them, walking towards the tiny flat that she shared with her father in the East End. Her pace was unusually slow. Coco and Zac caught up with her easily.

'Hey Sasha,' Zac greeted her as they drew alongside. Sasha looked up, surprised. Her face was tired. Her usual, default grin looked as though it was hard work today.

'Hey, you two, are you heading for the quays?' she said, hanging one arm over each of their shoulders, so that they could all walk together.

'Yup, usual spot.' Zac replied.

'You're late getting home,' Coco said, concern overcoming any suspicions about Sasha for a moment. 'Are you ok?'

'I hope you weren't held up at the café,' Zac said. He'd been there to try and help whenever he could to give her a break, but he knew that Sasha had been working really long hours to help Ed out while he was struggling.

'I had to stop at the chemist to get some medicine for my dad,' Sasha replied. 'My aunt is there at the moment, so I've got a couple of hours to spare. I thought I'd make the most of it and walk instead of getting the train.'

'Have you got time for a quick hot chocolate?' Zac said. 'We need to ask you something.'

'If you make it a coffee, you're on,' Sasha said.

'So, just to be clear,' Sasha said, as they slipped into the plastic chairs of their favourite fast food place on the quayside. 'Alannah told you that there was money missing and that Grace had seen me by the till, at lunch time.'

'Yup,' Coco said, 'but it's OK if you did take it, Sasha. We know you would pay it back. We know how difficult things are at home with your dad not able to work, and you having to look after him and pay all the bills, and study and everything all at the same time. We understand.'

'And it's okay if you took the comic, too. Your dad's health is more important than a comic. Even that one,' Zac said. 'And it is valuable. We just found out that it may be more valuable than everyone thought. We know that you would only have taken it if you were really, really desperate,' Zac added.

Sasha's face seemed to cycle through a hundred different emotions. When they had first suggested she might have stolen from them, she had looked hurt and angry and upset and as though she couldn't decide whether to cry or run or shout at them – and then, just as quickly, when she heard them pre-emptively forgive her, and be so understanding and kind and sweet, she knew that Zac and Coco, this whole family, were so precious to her that she forgave them, and looked touched and happy that they would have such a difficult conversation with her. She knew it must have been really hard for both of them.

Coco and Zac were looking nervously at her while she wiped away tears. Had they messed things up again? Neither of them really thought Sasha could be the thief – of the money or the comic – but the last few days had been so confusing that they really weren't feeling very sure about anything at the moment.

'Thanks for being so understanding, both of you, but I didn't take the comic and I didn't take the money either.' Sasha paused. 'I might be desperate, but I'm not a thief. I don't suppose that Alannah mentioned the note that I left to say that I had taken fifty pounds of change for the café because I couldn't get out to the bank and we'd run out of pound coins?' she asked.

'No, she didn't …' Zac said slowly.

'Interesting,' Sasha said. 'I wonder why not?'

'Why not what?' Coco asked, her attention stolen by the huge amount of whipped cream and marshmallows on the hot chocolate, which had just arrived.

Zac filled her in. 'Sasha left a note about the missing money in the till at Cosmic. She took it because the café needed change.'

'I'm just confused about why Alannah told you about the missing money, but not the note. It seems a bit strange,' Sasha said.

'Maybe the note had slipped down the back of the till, like the book tokens do sometimes?' Zac said.

'Yup, makes sense. She probably just didn't see it,' Coco agreed.

'It's possible,' Sasha said thoughtfully. 'But unlikely. I left the note in the change compartment at the front of the till drawer. It was under the coins and it would be hard to miss when you're cashing up.'

Downing the rest of her coffee, Sasha threw her jacket back on. 'Come on, you two, we're going back there now. If the note isn't down the back of the till, then Alannah saw it – and if she's seen it and not told you, something else is going on and I want to know what.'

Zac and Coco had to run to catch her up this time. They made it back to Cosmic in half the time it had taken earlier. Sasha unlocked the front door and walked to the cash desk without bothering to turn any lights on. There was just enough glow from the late evening sun to make out their way across the shop.

Sasha reached under the desk for the secret catch to spring open the till drawer. The drawer shot out, sending every nearby object crashing to the floor.

Coco ran around to help her pick up a pot of pens, a pile of paper bags and the ultra violet scanner for checking bank notes are real.

'Stop!' Zac shouted suddenly as Coco grabbed the scanner. 'Don't move.'

Coco froze. 'What is it? Is there someone there?'

'No, it's the UV light,' Zac said. 'Turn it back, and make it point down the stairs into the gallery. Exactly where it was before you touched it.'

Sasha stood up to see what he was looking at. 'Oh my god,' she gasped. 'There's a message on the covers of the comics.'

'What?' Coco said. 'Where? I want to see!'

Sasha took the scanner from her and held it in the same position, shining ultra violet light down into the gallery room where all Zac's remaining limited edition Komodo Jones comics hung in frames on the walls.

Shining out, under the purple light of the scanner, on each and every comic cover, appeared the words: 'From Z to Z.'

'Your mum organised for those special editions to be sent to you every six months, Zac, but they must really have come direct from Zander Cooper. They're from your dad!'

'Whaaaaat?' Sasha dropped the scanner in surprise. 'What do you mean, they're from Zander Cooper and they're from your dad? What have your dad and Zander Cooper got to do with each other?'

'Oh, with the money missing and everything, we forgot to tell you. We found Zac's birth certificate earlier,' Coco said, 'His real dad is *the* Zander Cooper.'

'He is not my *real* dad! How many times –' Zac asked, looking crossly at Coco.

'Real or unreal dad! That's crazy!' Sasha said. 'Anyway, how can you know that it's *the* Zander Cooper and not just any old Zander Cooper?'

'We've been through that,' Zac replied. 'Zander's full name is on the birth certificate and his middle name is Isaac, which is my full name. And the whole comic thing … weird as it is. I don't think it's a coincidence …'

'Zac!' Coco had grabbed a UV pen from the Galaxy section and was studying the covers up close in case there was anything else hidden there. 'Remember: just before Alannah interrupted us, you were about to think about where the phone number was.' Coco caught Sasha's quizzical look. She explained, 'We think that the original comic contains some kind of message from Zander Cooper to Zac. There was a phone number hidden in something in the story. We just need him to remember.'

'I think I've got it,' Zac said, without much enthusiasm. 'It was hidden in a barcode. The barcode that was on the back of a reference book on amphibians that Komodo's husband gave to her just before he escaped through the basement.'

'That man is a genius!' Sasha said.

'Thanks,' Zac replied.

'Not you! Zander Cooper! What a great place to hide a number!' Sasha looked really impressed.

'But it doesn't help now,' Zac said. 'The comic has gone and so has the number.'

'But these comics, here,' Coco said, 'Why put this Z to Z message on these ones if there's nothing else there?'

'It's a bit odd just to let you know that he's sending them and then not giving you a way to contact him,' Sasha pointed out.

'It's all too weird and too complicated. I don't want to contact him!' Zac said, slumping back into his favourite chair. 'I don't need him. He left me, and Ed looked after me. I'm not about to phone some stranger up after thirteen years to ask for money. Even to save the building from redevelopment.'

'You might not need him,' Sasha said, 'but he needs you. I know this is all really hard on you, Zac, but the press will just go for the headline that will sell the most papers and *Superhero-creating father abandons son* does not look good.' Sasha said.

'Well, it's the truth,' Zac replied.

'I'm sure that he had his reasons. Sometimes people leave because they do love someone, not because they don't. I'm sure that he and your mum did what they believed was going to be best for you,' Sasha said.

'A barcode on the back of a book,' Coco muttered to herself, thinking out loud. 'Maybe that was a clue too!' She grabbed a stool and pulled it over to the first framed comic.

Hopping up on to the stool, Coco unhooked the first frame, jumped down and lay it on the table. She moved the stool over and hopped up for the next one.

'What are you doing?' Zac stood up to try to stop her. 'You're going to drop one. Stop being crazy, there's enough stuff to deal with, without you messing up the comics!'

'The barcodes,' Coco said, ignoring him and reaching up for the next one, 'Check the barcodes on the front of each of these comics.'

'That could be it!' Sasha said, starting to take the comics out of their frames and laying them out.

Reluctantly, Zac joined her. 'Give them to me, Coco. You'll crack the glass.'

All three of them stood, reading out the numbers on the barcodes on the front cover of each issue. They wrote them down and it became immediately clear that every single one of them had an identical barcode.

'But they're different editions,' Zac said. 'That's not possible. Every edition has to have its own unique barcode. Check them again, we've missed something, a two that looks like a five. Something!'

'They're all the same! We've checked over and over,' Coco said, 'It must be *the number*. The emergency number for Zac to call Zander Cooper. Just like in the original version of *Komodo*.' Coco took his phone out of his pocket and handed it back to him. 'Call it, Zac.'

'No, *thanks*.' Zac put the phone down on the table.

'Fine! I'll do it.' Coco picked the phone up and dialled the number. She held the phone up so they could hear. 'I'm just getting a weird tone. I don't think it is a number. It's not connecting through to anything.'

'See. This number thing is all in your head. If by some miracle there was a contact number, it was in the original and it's gone.'

Coco ignored him and dialled again. 'Damn! Just a weird tone again!'

'Zac, there is the possibility that it's an American number,' Sasha said gently, seeing how much Zac was hating every second of this. 'How about we give it one more try with the dialling code and then give up?'

'I don't seem to have much choice,' Zac said,

nodding to Coco who was already looking up the dialling code at the cash desk.

Zac dialled it, slouching back down so low in the red leather chair that he was almost part of it. Pressing each number seemed to require the effort of a weight lifter.

'Put it on speaker!' Coco said. 'I want to hear.'

Zac pressed the speaker button just as the answer phone kicked in.

'Hi, if you've reached this number, you must be Zac. If you're not Zac, you have the wrong number. Please hang up. If you are Zac, hello and please leave me a number. I will call you back the second that I can.'

The message finished. Zac hung up.

'What are you doing?' Coco tried not to yell at him, but couldn't keep her voice below a screech. 'You didn't leave a message.'

'I didn't know what to say.'

'Of course you didn't.' Sasha came and sat next to him, perching on the arm of the chair. 'Who would know what to say after just finding out that their biological dad is the creator of one of the top comic superheroes, and your own personal favourite – a famous recluse, who left you a personalised hand-drawn comic partly explaining why he had to leave and then sent you a comic every month with a phone number on, especially for you! It's not exactly a situation that life prepares you for.'

Perching on the other arm of the chair, Coco apologised for screeching at him. 'We could practise what you want to say before you dial it again. If you like.'

'No need. I'm not dialling it again,' Zac said. 'The whole thing is doing my head in.'

'Maybe just leave him your number,' Sasha said.

'That will be on his phone as a missed call,' Zac said. 'I don't need to call again.'

'He won't know that it's you, though,' Sasha said. 'It could have been anyone that called. Just name and number.'

Coco took the phone from him, dialled the number and handed it back to Zac just as the message played again.

Zac mumbled into the phone. 'Umm … Hi … It's … um … Zac …' He left his number as quickly as he could and hung up.

'Happy now? I've had to go through all this and we still don't know who took the comic and we are no closer to saving the café.' He looked at them both angrily before throwing his phone down on to the table and walking out of the front door.

KOMODO JONE

AND SAM WILSON IN...

KOMODO JONES: ON TRIAL

After Coco explained about her nine attempts to talk to Zac at school that day, and then four more in the café in the afternoon, Sasha gave Coco a sympathetic look that told her he was ignoring her, too, and he probably needed some space. Coco gave up and went back up to her flat. She prayed that Grace wouldn't be there. She didn't think that she could cope with Zac ignoring her and Grace on her case at the same time.

As she stepped cautiously into her flat, thinking how lucky she had been most of her life never to have been scared of coming into her own home – stupid Grace – the phone rang right next to her. She leapt into the air, whacked her elbow on a doorframe, and then answered the phone. It was an estate agent, phoning for Alannah. Coco offered to take a message, and realised when the man started giving it to her that she didn't have any paper within reach, so she scribbled it on her arm with the UV pen she still had in her back pocket. It would show up under the UV light, and she could write it down properly later on for Alannah.

She heaved a sigh of relief when she realised that Grace was nowhere to be seen. Coco opened the cupboard and reached up for the biscuit tin. It felt very light, which was strange as there had been a full packet of custard creams, half a packet of chocolate caramel digestives and two thirds of a packet of bourbons when she'd taken some for her packed lunch that morning.

She gave the tin a shake. Nothing. She took off the lid. Not a single biscuit. Just a note in a handwriting that she recognised as Grace's saying, 'Thought you'd like another kiddie game to play, so I've hidden all the biscuits for you. Happy biscuit hunting, little piggy!'

Coco took the note out and ripped it into tiny bits. Then she took the tiny bits and tore each and every one of them into even tinier bits. Then she took all the tiny bits and stamped up and down on them, grinding them into the floor. When she was tired of stamping, she scooped them up from the floor, walked to the bathroom and spotted the pot of lime and rose scented body scrub that she knew was Grace's favourite. Picking it up with one hand, she tucked it under her arm and took off the lid. After sprinkling the bits of paper inside, Coco gave it a good shake. When she saw that the paper couldn't be seen in the thick liquid, she got another idea. Grabbing the dustpan and brush from under the kitchen sink, she swept up the few bits of paper that she had dropped along with the layer of dust and crumbs from the floor that came with them. She spotted a cobweb forming in the corner and put that in to the dustpan too, and added in a dead fly from the windowsill. Then she tipped it all in to the body scrub and gave it a good stir with the bristle end of Grace's toothbrush, put the lid back on and placed it back, exactly where it had been.

Back in the kitchen, grinning to herself a little, Coco pulled all her school stuff out of her bag to start on her homework. One sentence in and she knew that she couldn't concentrate on anything except the case. After clearing a space on the table, she got her notebook from its hiding place under the sink and behind the washing up liquid – where she knew Grace wouldn't find it.

Taking her favourite pen from her bag, she started to look back over everything that they knew about the missing comic. She looked through all the pages of crossings-out and addings-in from the last few days, turned to a clean page and made a neat copy of the up-to-date information.

Suspects:

Sasha — knew the code, desperately needs money.

Alannah — pointed the finger at Sasha, makes her suspicious.

Grace — because I hate her. She's a troll and a horrible idiot.

Motives:

Sasha — Desperation.

Alannah — Not sure why but something's not right.

Grace — Because she's an evil alien.

Opportunity:

Sasha — has keys to the shop, knew the code and knows the comic is worth money (problem, wouldn't be able to sell it without it making the news).

Alannah — doesn't know the code and wouldn't be able to sell it. But was in the shop on the day that it went missing.

Grace — vile, vile two-faced vile vileness from Vileville. Would find a way to do it just because she's vile!

Other information:

Possible motive could be selling the story to the papers (less likely to be Sasha as she wouldn't have known about the link between Zac and Zander. But might have overheard a conversation between Ed and Emma at some point? Alannah might have known about Zander Cooper because of knowing Zac's mum in the band, but doesn't know the code and doesn't need the money).

'Damn it!' Coco thought. 'The information just

leads around in circles and then still points to Sasha. 'And we forgot all about the note in the till. I need to go back down and check whether Sasha is lying, or Alannah is.'

The note reminded Coco about the message for Alannah. She scanned the UV light end of her pen over her arm to check it was legible – 'Phew!'

Just as she was going into her mum's room for the sticky note pad that Emma kept next to her bed, she heard the front door going and Alannah and Grace's voices in the hall.

'You promised you'd take me to get my nail replaced,' Grace said angrily. 'It happened last Thursday and you still haven't taken me.'

'I've had a lot to do with the shop and everything,' Alannah said, 'I've just closed up early today *especially* to take you. Let me check that Coco is OK and then we can go.'

Unable to find the sticky note pad underneath all of Alannah's things that littered her mum's bedroom, Coco had just found a piece of paper on the bedside table and was holding it up to check that it was OK to write on. Glancing over it, she saw that it was a demand for late payment for Grace's school fees. They were two terms overdue.

'Coco?' Alannah called out as she came into the

room. Her face darkened when she saw what Coco was holding. Marching over, she snatched the letter from Coco. 'That's private! Why are you snooping around in my room?!'

'I'm so sorry,' Coco said, shocked. She had never seen Alannah like this before and the sudden change was unnerving. 'I just wasn't thinking and forgot that it's your room while Mum's away. Mum always lets me in here. I just came in to leave you a note.'

'Why didn't you leave the note in the kitchen?' Alannah's face remained hard and fixed.

'I wanted to make sure you got it. They said it was important,' Coco said. 'And it's written on my arm so I needed some paper.'

'Read it out,' Alannah said.

Coco felt like an idiot as she shone the UV light pen on her arm to read out the message, Grace glaring at her from the doorway.

Alannah scribbled the message down on the back of the fees letter. Coco glanced over at her to see whether she was calming down and noticed that she was writing with her left hand. Coco tried not to get distracted by this new information as she struggled to make out the last digit of the phone number. 'It's a two, definitely a two.'

KOMODO JONE

KOMODO JONES: UNDONE!

ISBN 978-1-909991-65-1

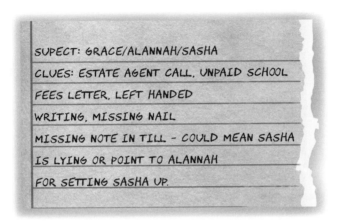

CHAPTER THIRTEEN

SUPECT: GRACE/ALANNAH/SASHA

CLUES: ESTATE AGENT CALL, UNPAID SCHOOL

FEES LETTER, LEFT HANDED

WRITING, MISSING NAIL

MISSING NOTE IN TILL – COULD MEAN SASHA

IS LYING OR POINT TO ALANNAH

FOR SETTING SASHA UP.

'I know you hate me,' Coco began, bursting out of the revolving door into the café kitchen and banging into Zac, 'but you have to listen. We have some new evidence to add to the list: Grace lost a nail last Thursday, Alannah owes money and she's left-handed and there was no note down the back of the till – I just found it in the bin under the cash desk at Cosmic ...' Coco tugged on Zac's arm.

'Stop it, you're going to make me drop them,' he said, pulling away and rebalancing the plate of scones he was carrying.

'But don't you see what this means, Zac? Alannah's got a motive: she owes loads of money. She's just behaved really strangely, and Grace said that Mum and I had ruined everything. Please, please, please can we just sit down with the evidence again?'

'OK,' Zac said, putting down the plate. 'But I haven't forgiven you for making me phone that number.'

'Has he called?' Coco asked.

'No.' Zac shook his head. 'Just give me a moment to help Sasha to lock up and I'll grab my backpack. The evidence tin is still in there.'

'Can I have one of these while I'm waiting?' Coco asked, looking lovingly at the scones, oozing cream and jam.

'Help yourself', Zac said, 'they have to be eaten today. But save a couple for Tom.' Coco took two scones and wrapped them up for Tom, the homeless guy who lived in the doorway of one of the empty shops on the parade. She poured him a flask of tea, too, before sinking her teeth into a scone herself. Jam and cream oozed down the front of her T-shirt. She finished it off, licked the crumbs from her T-shirt and zipped her hoodie up to cover the stains.

'I found the note you left in the till in the bin behind the cash desk,' Coco said to Sasha as she came into the kitchen to drop off some empty soup bowls. 'Why do you think Alannah didn't tell us about it?'

'That's what I've been wondering.' Sasha said. 'There's something about her and that spoilt daughter of hers that I just don't trust.'

'Me too now,' Coco said. 'She's always been so nice to me, giving me doughnuts and feeding me, but she found me with a letter about Grace's school fees being two terms overdue and changed into a completely different person.' Coco filled her and Zac in on what had happened upstairs, finishing with the part where Grace had said that Coco and Emma had ruined everything.

'You poor thing,' Sasha said to Coco, 'that must have been awful. What I'd like to do to that girl!'

'It does sound more and more like it might have been one of them,' Zac said, thoughtfully. 'And they were both around in the shop the evening that the comic went missing. But neither of them know the code, so I don't see how they could have taken it without setting the alarm off.'

'Remember how easily you guessed Ed's safe combination?' said Coco. 'What if she managed to somehow work out the code?'

'But it's just a random load of numbers, isn't it?' Zac said.

'But that's the point; maybe it's not random.'

'Hang on!' Sasha said to Coco, as though an idea had just occurred to her. 'Alannah was in the band with your mum, wasn't she?'

'Yup,' Coco said.

'And with your mum,' Sasha said to Zac.

'Yes,' Zac said from the sink where he had started loading the dishwasher.

'Codes ...' Sasha started and then paused, as if trying to work something out. 'There's a way that your Mum helped me to remember the code for the case,' Sasha continued. 'You remembered it by singing the first line of Pop Pow's biggest hit – Summer Rain.' Sasha took out her iPod and handed Zac and Coco an ear phone each. Scrolling through her playlist, she selected the right song, 'Listen carefully,' she said as the track began to play, '... Summer rain, falling again, blurring all my memories of you.' Sasha sang along, out of tune.

Coco and Zac had heard the song a thousand times on the radio. They could both have hummed it in their sleep if anyone had ever needed them to. They looked at Sasha blankly. Why was she was playing it to them?

'The notes,' Sasha said, singing the line to them again, 'ADDFAFBD ... when you work out their position in the alphabet, they give you the numbers of the code: A equals one, D equals four etc. Until you get the whole code: 14461724. I can't think why I didn't remember it before!'

'Don't worry, Sasha, there's been a lot going on!' reassured Coco. She picked up some dirty plates from the counter and began loading them into the dishwasher.

'That's so weird,' Zac said. 'Ed told me the code but he never mentioned where it had come from. I assumed it had just been the one programmed into the case when it was fitted!'

'So someone who was in the band with Mum, someone who knew her well enough to know how bad she was with remembering numbers, might be able to work out what code she would use?' Coco said, putting the clean plates on the shelves and handing Zac the dirty ones.

'Alannah!' they all said together.

'The very same person who would have been around long enough to possibly know who your biological dad was,' Sasha said.

'And the same person who owes lots of money,' Coco said. 'Let's go and find her! She might not have had time to go to the press since Mum's been away. She's been covering the shop a lot of the time, and she's hardly been out. The comic could still be somewhere nearby. We could still get it back in time to get money for the rent and save the block!'

Sasha and Zac grabbed the plates that Coco was holding to prevent her dropping them in her excitement.

'Even if it is her,' Zac said, putting in the last plate and closing the dishwasher, 'we can't just run in and accuse someone else. We've been wrong every time so far.' He looked guiltily at Sasha, who smiled reassuringly. 'We need some proof, some real, hard evidence.'

'Are you saying, are you actually saying, that we need to be patient ... again?!' Coco asked.

'Sorry, Coco, but yes,' Zac replied.

KOMODO JONE

AND SAM WILSON IN...

THE CASE OF THE UNSEEN

ISBN 978-1-909991-65-1

9 781909 991651

Walking out of a detention that they'd been given for passing notes in class that day, Coco and Zac talked over one another all the way home.

'I can't believe they kept us late just because of the note,' Coco said. 'Today of all days!'

'You did pass it to me in the middle of a test,' Zac said.

'It was a French test and the note was about the pair of left-handed scissors we found at the crime scene. It was written in English, so I clearly wasn't trying to cheat,' Coco protested.

'I think it was more about us not concentrating ...' Zac said.

'I *was* concentrating,' Coco said, 'just not on the stupid test! Learning French isn't going to get the comic back, and if we hadn't had to study for it last night, we might have solved this by now.'

'It would be so much easier if it was still half term,' Zac agreed. 'Every second that it takes us to get enough evidence to prove it was her is a second that

Alannah gets to finish off her plan.'

'We have to keep acting normal so we don't make Alannah suspicious that we are on to her,' Coco said. 'Otherwise, if she still has the comic, she might try to destroy it, so that there's no more evidence.'

'Destroying it would be even worse than her selling it to the press,' Zac said. 'I really don't want people to know who I am just because Zander Cooper happens to be my dad. Not that he seems to care: he hasn't even bothered to call back. But Mum gave me that comic. If I have to let it go, it's got to do some good.'

'We've got no time for homework tonight; we can't waste another nanosecond until we crack this case,' Coco said.

After begging Ed to write them each a note for the following day, explaining why they hadn't done that evening's homework, 'due to an important family occasion,' Zac and Coco left him alone and settled down at one of the café tables, spreading out the evidence in front of them.

'OK, we know that Alannah is left-handed, so that links her to the left- handed scissors found at the scene,' Zac said.

'What could she have been using the scissors for?' Coco asked. 'They would have left marks on the case, if she'd use them to try to break in.'

'I'm not sure, she could have been using them to open boxes or something to help your mum,' Zac said. 'It might have been something innocent but it does show that she was there around that time. No one else who works in the shop is left-handed.'

'The false nail matches the one that Grace was missing, so she was there around then too,' Coco added. 'I checked: silver and turquoise stripes.'

'Maybe that's why Grace didn't want us to show her in there last Thursday. Perhaps she had already taken it and didn't want us to find out while she was still there.'

'And it makes sense of why Alannah lied about the note from Sasha,' Zac said. 'Remember in *Komodo Jones and the Case of the Confused Identity*, Komodo says, "the person who points the finger, is always pointing in the same direction … away from themselves."'

'Exactly,' Coco said, 'Alannah must have been trying to give us even more reason to think it was Sasha.'

'To put us off suspecting *her*,' Zac finished.

'Or Grace,' Coco said.

'Do you think that Alannah and Grace are in on it together?' Zac asked.

'Now that I've seen the dark side of both of them, I wouldn't rule it out,' Coco said. 'Except that Grace can't keep quiet about anything. If she had something to gloat over, she would have spilled the beans by now!'

'We might have underestimated her,' Zac said. 'Grace was there on her own after we left her that first evening, waiting for Alannah to take her to her dance class. Alannah would have had to tell her the code, but then she could have taken it without anyone seeing.'

'And Alannah knew the code, but she didn't even come into the shop that night, did she? Grace said she texted her from the car. But then Grace is evil, so maybe she's lying? Either way, if Alannah did take it, Grace must have seen her.'

'Then they must both be in on it; it's the only thing that makes sense,' Zac said. 'But we've still got to prove it.'

'The camera!' Coco suddenly remembered. 'We haven't picked it up from the chemist.'

'I'll go,' Zac said. 'It's about to close and I'll be quicker on my own. Go through the timings again and see if you can think of anything else.'

Coco sat staring at the objects they had gathered, and drew a new timeline of the events of the past few days. She paced up and down, and then sat staring at the page with her fingers pressed up against her temples, to try to push the thoughts out. It didn't work. She then tried skipping up and down the room, and then hopping. Still nothing. She sat down again, and reviewed the page; it was still mostly question marks.

Coco piled the evidence back into the tin and threw it behind the counter in Zac's bag. Slipping through the rotating door, she walked down into the gallery.

'I'm just locking up,' Alannah called to her, back to her usual friendly self, 'and then I'm going to the office to cash up. Supper at eight; I'm making your favourite: macaroni cheese!'

'Thanks, Alannah. I'll check the back door is locked,' Coco called back as she walked to the back to check the locks.

On close inspection, Coco couldn't see anything that suggested the locks had been tampered with. She heard Alannah close the door to the small office behind the cash desk.

'What am I missing?' Coco asked herself as she looked around the gallery. She spotted the two space-moose heads. One on the left of the glass case, one on the right. The police had fingerprinted the case but found nothing. Coco leapt on to a stool and pulled herself up by the moose head on the left. That way, she could feel around the edge of the case with her right hand.

'That's it!' she thought, just as Zac came into the gallery. 'It's the moose!' she shouted at him.

'The moose took it?!' Zac said, looking seriously confused.

'No!' Coco leapt down. 'We need to fingerprint the moose.'

Zac didn't look any less confused.

'Alannah's really short, like me.' Coco explained in a whisper, remembering that Alannah was in the office within hearing distance. 'You know how I have to stand on the stool and pull myself up by the antlers to reach the buttons for the code. I've seen the cleaner do the same thing when she's polishing the glass on the case. Well, Alannah couldn't have got up there without doing that, too. We need to fingerprint the moose on the right-hand side – it will give us proof that she took it. The police didn't fingerprint the moose. I told Emma on the night of the theft that she should tell them to fingerprint it when they came, but they didn't see the point, apparently. No one but Alannah would have touched the moose on the right, because everyone else would use their right hand to key in the code. Only a left-handed short person would pull themselves up on the moose on the right!'

'I'll grab one of the kids' spy kits from the crime section!' Zac said as he ran for the stairs.

'The photos,' Coco called, suddenly remembering where Zac had been. 'What were they of?'

'They're in my jacket pocket; it's on the chair,' Zac called back over his shoulder.

'They're all of you,' Coco said when Zac came back.

'I know,' Zac answered, taking the lid off the kit.

'That's really creepy,' Coco said, unpacking the kit.

He nodded. 'It really is. Let's do this and then work out what the photos mean.'

Zac unfolded the instructions. He scanned past the headings: 'Using Rear View Glasses' and 'Seeing Around Corners', before pausing on 'Invisible Ink. I know all about that one, he thought. He'd given up on Zander ever returning his call and even though it made no real sense, he felt rejected again, by a dad that he had never known. He reached the section on taking fingerprints and started to read the instructions aloud for Coco to follow. After Coco accidentally emptied the first bag of dusting powder on to the floor, Zac handed her the instruction booklet to read out, so he could take over laying out the equipment.

'Number one,' Coco read. 'Dip the soft brush (any

soft make-up brush will do) into the dusting powder
(cocoa powder, talcum powder and icing sugar can
all be used for this) and brush lightly over the area
that you want to test. Start at the top and work down.
Number two ...'

'Hang on, I can't go that fast! We might miss
something, so slow down,' Zac said, still using the kit
brush to apply the dusting powder really carefully on
to every part of the antlers.

Coco waited until he'd finished and looked up for
the next instruction. 'Number two,' she continued.
'Take the clear sticky tape and place over the area you
want to take a print from. Press firmly to get rid of
any air bubbles.' Coco looked up at Zac, ' Have you
found any finger marks you can take a print from?'

'Yup, there's quite a clear set around the main part
of the antler,' Zac said, looking at it closely. 'It's just
going to be tricky to get the tape on all the finger
marks in one go.'

Coco held her breath as he tore off a wide piece of
tape and making sure that he only touched the ends,
placed it steadily on to the area with the prints.

'Press it firmly into place,' Coco reminded him.

'OK, that bit's all done,' Zac said as he finished.
'What's next?'

KOMODO JONES

AND SAM WILSON IN...

AND THE CASE OF THE WHISPERING WOL

ISBN 978-1-909991-65-1

9 781909 991651

CHAPTER FIFTEEN

Getting away after supper had been easy. As soon
as Coco and Zac had offered to wash up, Alannah
and Grace had both disappeared to their rooms.
Grabbing a plastic bag from a kitchen drawer, Zac
carefully turned it inside out and placed it over
Alannah's glass without touching the glass with his
hands. He found a different coloured bag and did
the same with Grace's glass.

'OK, don't forget,' he whispered to Coco, 'Alannah's
is in the red bag, Grace's in the blue bag; we mustn't
forget or we won't know which prints are whose.'

'Alannah red, Grace evil blue, Alannah red, Grace
evil blue' whispered Coco to herself.

Back down in the shop, Coco followed the
instructions to take prints from Grace's glass, while
Zac did Alannah's. They pulled out the prints
they'd taken from the antlers earlier, and laid them
alongside the new ones.

'Pass me the magnifying glass from the kit,' Zac said.

'Whose are they?' Coco asked, handing him the

magnifier. 'Whose prints match?'

'Just a sec,' Zac said, examining them more closely.

Coco tried to be patient, 'Alannah or Grace?' she asked again five seconds later.

'If you ask me again, I'm not going to tell you,' Zac said. 'I know our two choices!'

'OK, I'm pretty sure which ones match,' Zac said, handing Coco the magnifying glass. 'Now you look and see if we get the same answer, just to be sure.'

'The prints on the right! Definitely!' Coco said. She looked at the plastic bag that they had placed next to each glass to remind them. 'Alannah's! She's the thief!'

'And now,' said Zac, 'we've got evidence. The second that we get out of school tomorrow, we're going to confront her.

'But that gives her another whole day to do something with the comic,' Coco said, 'and I can't wait that long.'

'She has to be here all day tomorrow. Grace is at school, so she can't cover the shop for her and she usually gets home about twenty minutes after we do.'

If the night of the comic theft had been the longest night of their lives, this day had been the longest day. Coco had been told off in every lesson for clock watching. Zac had warned her at lunchtime that if she got another detention, they would be late back.

'I know,' Coco said, 'I'm trying so hard to concentrate, but it's as though my whole body keeps wanting to run home.'

'I feel the same way,' Zac said, 'but we've got to get through to the end of the day without getting into trouble, so please, for me, try even harder.'

Bursting out through the main doors of the school as the last bell went, Zac and Coco ran the entire way home.

The front door of Cosmic banged open as they pushed through it. Three customers queuing at the counter turned around to see what the commotion was. Coco looked around for Alannah and then went straight into service mode.

'Hello, is someone helping you?' she asked the first person in the queue.

'No they are not,' he replied, 'and I've been waiting here for at least ten minutes. If I didn't need this toy Batmobile, today, for my son's birthday, I would have walked out already. I could have stolen it ten times over, you know.'

'I'm so sorry,' Coco said, 'let me take that for you.' She rang it through the till, took the money and handed it back in one of their bright Cosmic paper bags. 'I hope your son has a lovely birthday,' she said as the man snatched the bag and marched out.

Coco served the next two equally annoyed customers while Zac looked all around the shop and then in the café, trying to find Alannah.

'It's been too long for her just to have gone to the toilet,' Coco said as Zac came back in. 'Where else could she be while the shop is open, anyone could have stolen anything in that time! Turn the sign in the door to "Closed" and I'll try the office,' Coco said, waiting for him before pressing down on the door handle. Zac was close behind her.

'Grace!' Coco said in surprise, recognising the back of her head. Grace had her feet up on the desk and was turning the pages of a comic with one hand and holding a nail varnish brush with the other. The pot of nail varnish was holding down the page of the comic to stop it from flipping over while she read.

'Hello,' Grace drawled in a disinterested voice without turning around.

'Where's your mum?' Coco asked. 'She's supposed to be covering the shop?'

'Oh, she had some urgent, super-important meeting to go to, so I bunked off school for the afternoon so I could do the shop thing for her, but then I got bored, so I came in here. This was the only thing I could find to read – God it's dull!' Grace picked up the comic with her newly-painted nails.

'Oh my God!' Zac recognised it instantly and pushed past Coco to get into the office, 'That's the comic! Grace, please, you've got to put it down, you're going to get nail varnish on it.'

'How did you get that?' Coco demanded as she too realised what Grace was dangling in mid air.

'Not now, Coco!' Zac said. 'Grace, please, I am begging you, however much you hate us, whatever you and your mum are planning on doing with it, just please, please put it down.'

'What, this old thing?' Grace asked, putting down the nail varnish brush so that she could hold the comic with both hands. 'What on earth would I want to do with this old thing?' She waved it just out of his reach.

'Grace, *that's the stolen comic!*' Coco yelled.

'Don't be stupid, Coco.' Grace said, '*The stolen comic* has been stolen. We all know that; it's all anyone ever talks about around here! This one was inside this horribly outdated fashion magazine, right here – you're just trying to make me look stupid.'

'Just hand it over, Grace. Please!' Zac begged.

'I don't think so,' Grace said, holding it further

over the desk on the other side of her as Zac reached out. 'Want it?' Grace waved it past his hands.

'Nooooo!' Zac and Coco both screamed with horror as Grace rammed the comic as hard as she could into the paper shredder under the desk.

'Can't have it!' she finished. 'That serves you right for trying to trick me ...' She pushed the last bit through.

Coco and Zac had frozen, shocked. The whole thing had seemed to happen in slow motion and also still be happening – but it wasn't. It was over. The comic was gone.

'*What have you done?!*' Coco and Zac turned to see Alannah standing behind them in the doorway. 'You stupid girl! That was *the* original, hand-drawn comic – our only chance of getting out of this dump. You've ruined everything I had worked out for us. The newspaper will only pay to publish the story with that comic as evidence, and now you've destroyed it!'

Grace broke down. Tears streamed down her face as she sobbed. For a second, Coco thought that Grace might apologize to Zac, but instead Grace shouted at her mother. 'Why didn't you tell me what you were doing, then? How was I supposed to know? It just looked like any other stupid comic!'

'Well it wasn't!' Alannah shouted at her. 'It wasn't

just any comic; it was the comic that was going to pay your school fees and buy the house with the swimming pool, and now we have nothing. Absolutely *nothing!*'

'So it was you,' Zac said slowly to Alannah. 'We were right.'

'Yes,' she spat, 'but you'll never be able to prove it. The comic has never left the shop, so the police aren't going to be interested. I hid it in plain sight, where you lot wouldn't be tempted to look. It technically wasn't even stolen; its been here the whole time.'

But how did you take it?' Grace asked, still trying to work out how this had suddenly all gone so wrong. 'When?'

'When I collected you for your dance lesson last Thursday, I let you in the car and came back inside alone, so I could 'check everything was properly locked,' Alannah said. 'I thought that would be my only chance. If I'd known that your mother was going to leave me in charge of the whole place for all this time, it would have made my life much easier! Anyway, nothing anyone can do about me taking it now.'

'But we've got fingerprints,' Coco said, 'from the space-moose.'

'Don't be ridiculous,' Alannah screeched. 'You're two kids. Who's going to believe you over me? It's just your word against mine.'

Silently, Zac took Coco by the arm and led her past Alannah, out of the office, across the shop, over to the secret doorway.

'And don't think your doorway is so secret,' Alannah called across to them in a voice that could freeze an ocean. 'I was here, watching you, from before that first evening. I came here disguised as a comic fan for months before I took the comic; I even took photographs to sell to the papers. I've seen everything.'

Coco reached up for the droid.

KOMODO JONE

AND SAM WILSON IN...

THE CASE OF THE THOUSAND EYES

ISBN 978-1-909991-65-1

Zac and Coco had found Sasha clearing up in the café as they hoped. They told her everything. She made plans for her aunt to look after her dad for a bit so that she could stay with them for as long as possible. Zac was in pieces. Coco and Sasha sat either side of him at the counter, their arms all touching, wishing they had the power to stop him from hurting.

Suddenly, he pulled something out of his backpack, and handed it to Coco.

'It's the voice activated robot thing.' She pressed the speaker button. '... You're two kids. Who's going to believe you over me? It's just your words against mine ...'

'It was in your backpack the whole time! It's recorded everything that Alannah said!' Coco yelped.

'Ssssh! Tomorrow ...' Zac said quietly.

'Tomorrow.' Coco and Sasha agreed.

When Sasha had to go, Coco and Zac went up to Zac's flat. Ed had gone to sleep early, as he seemed to most nights at the moment, so Zac and Coco sat in the kitchen, talking very quietly about what had just happened so as not to disturb him. Neither of them knew what to do next, but they had decided that Coco should stay at Zac's flat that night until they worked something out.

Zac and Ed had still not talked. The odd word here and there, but they hadn't had a conversation for almost a week now. There was so much to say, on both sides, but Zac was still trying to organise his thoughts, and Ed just seemed … broken. 'As soon as this is solved,' thought Zac, 'I need to get him a holiday'.

When Zac finally, reluctantly, woke up the next morning, he pulled the duvet back over his head and curled up into a ball. He remembered the time just after his mum had died and how he had to drag himself unwillingly through each day, hoping that the next one might be easier. Eventually, it had been. He knew that nothing would ever be that bad again, but he felt completely powerless now and even more alone. Ed had betrayed him. Emma must have known, too, he now realised. Everyone seemed to know more about him than he did. He had given up all hope of Zander calling back – and now with the comic gone, his home and the café, and Coco's home and shop, were gone too.

When even his duvet couldn't keep the daylight from creeping into his eyes, Zac rolled over and reached for his phone to check the time. He knew that he couldn't get to school today, and wondered whether they'd called Ed yet to check where he was.

His hand felt something on top of his phone on the bedside table. Opening his eyes as little as he could, he squinted across to pick it up. He was sure that it hadn't been there before. Opening his eyes fully, he ran his hand over the front of the cover. It's impossible, he thought ... It can't be. He shook his head. He felt awake, grim, but awake. He looked back at the comic in his hands – it was still there. He turned over the first page ... part of it had been inked in. It was exactly like his version of *the* comic. The comic that been shredded the day before. Exactly the same, but with colour.

Unwilling to put it down but desperate for someone to tell him that he wasn't imagining it, he ran out of his room to find Coco, still clutching the comic. He heard voices in the kitchen. 'Coco?' he called.

'We're in here, Zac.' Zac heard Ed's deep, comforting voice and headed for the kitchen. There was a tall, bearded stranger sitting at the table. 'Um, where's Coco?' Zac asked, his brain not working fast enough to cope with any more information.

'Zac,' Ed came over to give him a hug. 'I'm sorry. For lots of things, but especially the last few days. I've been a bit lost, and I know you needed me, but I couldn't snap out of it. Sasha called and filled me in on everything. I know that you know that I knew about Zander. I'm so sorry – you and Coco have had so much to deal with.'

'Is Coco here?' Zac wasn't sure how he felt about Ed yet. He needed somebody safe near him.

'She's still asleep, on the sofa. I've called the school to let them know that neither of you will be in today,' Ed said.

Zac looked across at the stranger and suddenly, with a sharp jolt, realised that he recognised him from the recent internet images he and Coco had seen from Comic-Con

'Zac,' Ed said, gesturing to the familiar looking stranger, 'this is Zander Cooper.' He put a plate of generously buttered crumpets and some milky coffee down in front of Zac, 'I'll leave you two to talk.' Ed squeezed Zac's shoulder reassuringly and kissed the top of his head, 'Love you, son,' he said as he left.

'Hello, Zac.' Zander smiled at him, 'I hear you've had a rough couple of days. Amazing detective work. I should start a new comic about you two Super Sleuthers!' he joked gently.

'Hello,' Zac said. 'Umm,' he shook his head. Sasha was right, nothing prepared you for leaving a message for a dad you didn't know you had, and absolutely no guide books told you what to say to one when you met him.

'It's OK,' Zander looked at him kindly, 'this was never going to be easy.'

'Did you leave this in my room?' Zac finally managed to look at Zander.

'Yes,' Zander said, 'it's the only other version of the comic; no one ever knew about it. I kept it as a reminder of you and your mum. It's yours now. I heard what happened to the other one.'

Zac nodded. 'Umm ... thank you.' He paused again, then asked, 'How did you know to come here? Did Coco's mum find you, or did you get my message?'

'Both,' Zander said. 'I'm so sorry that it took me so long to reply. I used to check for messages from you every day, after your mum died; but then no call came for years, so it dropped down to once a week, and then once a month. I never stopped thinking about you, or her, not ever, but I did stop checking.

I'm sorry. By the time that I did check, Emma had finally managed to get to me at Comic-Con to tell me she thought someone was about to sell the story about us. I knew that I needed to be here with you to deal with it if it happened. I got your message as I was getting on the plane late last night, and then couldn't use my phone. And now I'm here, instead.'

'At least there's one good thing about the comic being shredded: they can't sell the story now. So, you can be happy about that.' Zac said, avoiding looking at him again.

 'I'm not happy about any of this, Zac,' Zander said. 'You've been through hell and I haven't been here to help you. The only good thing about all of this is that I get to meet you. I've always wanted to have a chance to explain why I left.'

Zander talked, and Zac listened , for over an hour before Ed returned. By the time that he walked back into the kitchen, the atmosphere had fully thawed.

 'So, how are we all in here?' Ed asked cheerily. 'Ready for some more coffee? Oh, morning Coco,' Ed said, noticing a very crumpled-looking Coco with her duvet still around her shoulders at the kitchen door, 'your mum is back – she was trying to stay awake to see you, but didn't want to wake you.

She's in your flat, hopefully asleep, but she said to wake her whenever you're ready. I'll toast some more crumpets for you.'

Coco climbed on to a chair at the table, and grinned sleepily at Zac, 'No school!'

Zac smiled and passed his crumpet over to her. 'This is Zander. Zander, this is Coco.'

'Hi Coco,' Zander shook her hand, 'I've heard so much about you, I feel as though we've met.'

'Well, I know pretty much everything the internet knows about you!' Coco beamed at him. 'I can't believe that you're actually in Zac's kitchen!'

'Ed!' Zac remembered suddenly and turned to his step-dad, 'What are we going to do about the café and Cosmic and the rest of the block? You and Coco's parents were the last ones stopping the landlord, and now we've got no way to pay the rent. They're going to knock it all down.'

'I've got an idea about that,' Zander said.

'Can you buy the block?' Coco asked.

'Coco!' Zac glared at her.

'I'd love to,' Zander said, 'but apart from the small bit that I live on and a bit that I put aside for Zac for when he's 21, all the rest of the money – from the

Komodo comics and the Land Dragon books and film – goes to a charitable foundation to fund projects to help people. I don't want to take more than I need when there are people out there who are hungry.'

'So what's your idea then?' Coco asked, wondering what other options there could possibly be.

'It's something that I need to talk to Zac about first,' Zander said, turning to Zac. 'Fancy a walk around the block?'

'I should probably go and say 'hi' to Mum anyway?' Coco said, shoving the last of the freshly-toasted crumpets into her mouth and smiling at them all. 'Nice to meet you, Zander Cooper. See you later, Zac. Thanks for breakfast, Ed!'

Moments later, Coco stuck her head back round the door, 'Before I go down there; they have really gone, haven't they?'

'I promise,' Ed said. 'I can guarantee that Alannah and Grace will not be setting foot within ten miles of here again! I've never seen your mum like that before – I'm amazed you two slept through the yelling! But I'll come down with you and check for baddies myself before you go in, just to make sure.'

'Thanks Ed,' Coco followed him out.

KOMODO JONES

AND SAM WILSON IN...

THE CASE OF THE ILLEGAL LIZARD TRADE
PART TWO

ISBN 978-1-909991-65-1

9 781909 991651

While Zac filled Zander in on most of his life during their walk around the block, Coco found her mum. She climbed on to the bed next to her, and found out what had happened to Alannah. Emma had believed Sasha immediately when she'd called. It all made sense: the greed and revenge, the code and the lies, but the police had said that even with the taped confession, as the comic hadn't left the building, no crime had actually been committed. Alannah had been right about that, at least.

'So nothing happens to her?' Coco asked. 'She just gets away with it? '

'It may not be the punishment that she deserves, but it is the punishment that will be the worst for her. She's got nothing now, no us and no money. She might actually have to get a proper job!' Emma said as she wrapped Coco up in a huge hug. 'I'm so sorry you had to go through all this. I should have listened to you about Grace.'

Zac finished the tour at his and Coco's favourite spot on the roof of the building.

'I wanted to tell you why I had to leave you,' Zander said, as they stood admiring the view across the river. He waited for Zac to nod before he carried on. 'I loved your mother so much and we wanted to have a baby. But your mum was living the pop star life then and I didn't want the press following us, so I stayed hidden. When they found out that your mum was pregnant, they wanted to know who the father was, and then everything about me. We would wake up in the morning and there would be photographers on the doorstep, and hiding behind trees. I knew that I couldn't stay hidden for much longer, and I started feeling as though I couldn't breathe. I didn't want your mum to have to choose between me and the band, so I just left one day. I thought it would be better for both of you, better than me staying and making everyone miserable.'

'But she gave up the band anyway,' Zac said, confused.

'I know,' Zander said. 'I should never have gone.'

'I'm sure you're working this out,' continued Zander, 'but adults don't always do the right thing, even if they're trying to'.

Zac looked at the ground, not quite sure what to say or feel yet. 'It's not all bad,' he said finally, 'I have Ed and Coco and Emma and Sasha.'

'I know and, having met them, they're an amazing gang to have. No one would want to lose what you have here. Which is what made me think,' Zander started again, 'and its no small decision,' he paused, 'but perhaps it would be a good idea to sell the story about us to the press ourselves.'

'But you hate publicity,' Zac said. 'Despite what Coco said about you on the internet, no one knows anything much about you, except that!'

'I *really* hate publicity,' Zander said, 'but it's different now. This story is going to come out one way or another. I don't want us to live in fear of it happening. If we sell it ourselves, we get to tell it our way, to tell them about how great your mum was, and what a brilliant step-dad Ed has been, and how we will now be part of each others' lives. I mean ... if that's what you want?'

Zander looked at Zac. Zac nodded.

'This way, it's your story, and you've got the power to use the money to do something good for lots of people. Not just to pay the rent, but to actually do up the whole block.' Zander finished.

'I don't understand,' Zac said.

'The landlord can't knock the block down as long

as Ed and Em can pay their shop rent,' Zander explained. 'It's written into his lease. All he can do is keep on putting the rent up, and there are limits to that. If the landlord thinks he can't develop the block, he's not going to want it anymore. By law, all of the residents can get together and buy the block and manage it themselves. We just need to raise the money. Then imagine what you could do with it … It could be out of this world, amazing!' Zander finished.

Zac began to imagine …

Appearing in a lightning bolt, he'd zoom in, saving The Comic Café and Cosmic, and their flats, and Sasha and Josh's parent's jobs, and all of their homes, and the art school and the other shops. He'd paint the whole block like a giant comic. Stories would flow around the walls. In a flash, the empty shops would become a comic cinema. The broken-down playground would transform into a comic- themed play area and a planetarium! And … crowds of people would come from across the world to see it all, and to learn and draw and play and create …

'Zac?' Zander said. 'Earth to Zac – what do you think?'

'OK.' Zac shook himself out of the clouds and grinned. 'Yes! Let's do this! But first, I need to see Coco.'

Within minutes, Zac was hunting every corner of Cosmic for Coco. When he'd dropped into her flat on his way down from the roof, Emma had said that Coco had gone down to find him. After looking under dinosaurs, behind chairs and round superhero cut-outs, he headed for the revolving door to try the café.

'Why isn't this working?' he wondered to himself as he pulled on the droid again. The door stayed in place. 'Not now!' Zac thought. He tried again. Had Alannah managed to break it, just for an extra bit of meanness? The door refused to move. Zac gave it a shove, and was about to give up and go to the front door when he heard a rustling sound on the other side, 'Coco, is that you?' he called through the shelves.

'Zac! Yes! It is!' Coco shouted back. 'I've been looking for you! I've got cakes! The door won't work.'

'I think we've been trying it at the same time!' Zac said. 'Try it now and see what happens.'

There was a click and the door swung around. Coco stepped into Cosmic as Zac stepped out into the café. 'We didn't think that one through properly!' he laughed. 'Stay back from the door, I'm coming back round,' he called.

'Hey!' Coco greeted him, 'I ate one of the doughnuts I got for you, I couldn't wait any longer, but we can share this one. I need to hear everything!'

'I've got tons to tell you, but first this ...' he took the doughnut from Coco, and handed her the comic that Zander had left by his bed.

'No wayyyyyy!' Coco looked up at Zac in astonishment. 'It's like seeing a ghost comic!'

'And this ...' Zac held out the extended special edition *Komodo Jones* from the previous Thursday's delivery. 'We never got a chance to read it.'

Curled up in the battered red leather chair in the gallery, Coco turned the pages while they read. Zac perched on the arm of the chair next to her. They read and read, not stopping until they reached the last page of the Komodo special.

'The end,' Coco said as she closed the comic. 'That was definitely worth waiting for!'

'Thanks Coco,' Zac said.

'What for?' Coco asked. 'For leaving you some doughnut? Another ten seconds and I wouldn't have.'

'For being right – about it being the beginning – and not the end,' Zac said.

Tamara Macfarlane is a children's author and owner of the children's independent bookshop Tales on Moon Lane. She recently set up Moon Lane Ink CIC, a not-for-profit company promoting equality in children's books. As well as judging book prizes, Tamara has talked and performed at many festivals, both in the UK and internationally. She lives in London with her partner and children.

Eugene Ramirez Mapondera is an animator and illustrator based in Harare, Zimbabwe. He works remotely on international projects ranging from film, print, commercials and animated Films. He has been working closely with the Troika team to bring Komodo Jones to life as the book's principle artist.

Eugene is the co-founder of Comexposed, The Zimbabwean Comic Book Convention and is constantly pursuing the growth of gender diversity and tribal diversity in young people's literature in Zimbabwe and Africa as a whole.

Comic Shop Mysteries Book Two

The Unspoken Truth

FEATURING *KOMODO JONES*

While COSMIC comic shop and café are being rebuilt, Coco and Zac are sent off to stay with Zac's dad in America.

His epic mountain retreat is even more extraordinary than they could have imagined. The perfect place for the creation of their favourite comic strip super- hero: Komodo Jones! When the pair enter a comic competition ahead of the biggest Comic- con in the world, the mystery really begins. Can Coco and Zac solve this confusing crime and find the villain in the middle of thirty thousand people ... all in disguise?

This second book in the page-turning Comic Shop Mystery series follows another adventure of Coco and Zac and their crime-fighting friendship. Illustrated by the brilliant Eugene Ramirez Mapondera, the comic strip of Komodo Jones also continues, deepening the mystery of her past, her present and her future.

The Pedagogy of Creativity

The Pedagogy of Creativity represents a groundbreaking study linking the pedagogy of classroom creativity with psychoanalytical theories. Taking a classroom-based example of poststructuralist methodology as its starting point, Anna Herbert's investigation explores the relationship between creativity seen in psychological activity, such as dreams, and creativity seen in the classroom, asking the following questions:

- What might a methodology which taps into different forms of creativity look like?
- Could such a methodology support current neuropsychological theories of memory and learning?
- What are the consequences of imaginary and symbolic orders of knowledge for the understanding of both conscious and unconscious creativity in the classroom?

Exploring the ideas of a number of psychological analysts including Jacques Lacan's four discourses, concepts of 'the Other' and the theories of thinkers such as Levinas, Buber, Mead and Kristeva, Herbert explains how different theories can be used to develop creativity in the classroom and surmount obstacles preventing creative environments.

Clearly presenting both theoretical positions and their bearing on classroom practice, teachers at all levels will benefit from this innovative approach to creativity, as will school psychologists and all professionals interested in the links between psychoanalysis and pedagogy.

Anna Herbert works in the Department of Education, Lund University and Linneus University, Sweden.